TEENAGE TIMBERWOLVES

LUST FOR LIGHTNING

TEENAGE TIMBERWOLVES: LUST FOR LIGHTNING
DANIELE SERRA & JAMES HAVOC
ISBN 978-1-8383595-4-6
PUBLISHED BY BONEFYRE BOOKS 2023
COPYRIGHT © BONEFYRE BOOKS 2023
ALL WORLD RIGHTS RESERVED
https://bonefyrebooks.com

CONTENTS

FOREWORD

As a rabid collector and historian of classic Italian film poster art – especially in the horror genre – my eye has inevitably been drawn in recent years to the stunning graphic work of another, more contemporary artist from Italy: Daniele Serra. Daniele has illustrated a number of comics – most famously for Clive Barker's **Hellraiser** – and many striking and haunting book covers. But perhaps his strangest, and strongest, visual creation was the Hellscape conjured up by author James Havoc for the graphic novel **Teenage Timberwolves: Lust For Lightning**, first published a few years ago and long sold out.

It is a great pleasure, therefore, to write this foreword for the definitive, comprehensive edition of this wild work of horror and perversion. The new edition collects all texts relating to the **TTW** project – some from a now-defunct promotional website – as well as an appendix in the form of **Black Dead Bones Of Idiot Bill**, a 4-page black and white segment first published in a Lovecraftian anthology. On pages 26 to 28 of **TTW**, the seemingly immortal Billy Timberwolf regales his girl ghouls with tales from his long-distant past; **Idiot Bill** is one such tale, set in times of post-civil-war chaos.

Mixing elements that range from classic literature (the Marquis de Sade) to pop culture and celebrated true crime cases like those of Charlie Starkweather and Charles Manson, and blitzing them into a mythic vortex of abject madness, **TTW** is like nothing else I have ever read. It repulses and attracts on levels both blatant and occult, and the result still blows my tiny mind.

I do not profess to know what demons (beer demons, maybe?) drove Havoc to create the bizarre and twisted world of **TTW**, or how Daniele Serra was able to transmute his words into such vivid vistas of beautiful horror; but I remain truly thankful that they did.

G.H. JANUS
(editor, **Voluptuous Terrors** series)

THE TEENAGE TIMBERWOLVES

GUILLAUME GAROU, aka BRISE-CUL, aka ASS-DESTROYER, aka BILLY THE WOLF BOY, aka BILLY TIMBERWOLF, born 1772: SUN, SWASTIKA, EXCREMENT, GUN, BLACK. WANTED IN THIRTEEN STATES FOR VAGRANCY, GRAVE-ROBBING, CANNIBALISM, MURDER, AND SEVEN HUNDRED COUNTS OF SODOMY WITH A CORPSE.

CARIL COVEN, aka FIRESKIN, aged 23: MOON, SCORPIO, SPERM, KNIFE, SILVER. WANTED IN SEVEN STATES FOR MURDER, CANNIBALISM, ABETTING A RUNAWAY, AND SEXUAL INTERCOURSE WITH THUNDERBOLTS.

YUKI YUREI, aged 19: SATURN, CHAOS, BLOOD, SWORD, VERMILLION. WANTED IN THREE STATES FOR MURDER, CANNIBALISM, AND SEXUAL INTERCOURSE WITH THUNDERBOLTS.

CANDICE CARRION, aged 15: ALGOL, CRUX, TEARS, BIBLE, GOLD. WANTED IN THE STATE OF ALABAMA FOR JUVENILE DELINQUENCY AND ABSCONDING FROM CUSTODIAL CARE.

THE SUPPORTING CAST

DELILAH: SHE MAY BE JUST A DOLL MADE OF STITCHES AND SAWDUST, BUT INSIDE DELILAH THE SPIRIT OF CARIL'S MOTHER IS CAGED, SQUIRMING WITH AN INSATIABLE LUST FOR DEAD SOULS.

DR. LAZARUS LE FANU: GRANDSON OF ALCIBIADES LE FANU, CO-FOUNDER OF THE KNIGHTS OF THE WHITE CAMELIA, HE IS ALSO DIRECTOR OF THE WHITE CAMELIA MENTAL INSTITUTE, LOUISIANA. RUMOURED TO POSSESS THE LARGEST LIBRARY OF SNUFF MOVIES IN AMERICA, HIS ROLE MODELS ARE JOSEF MENGELE AND POL POT.

THE NURSES: GONZALEZ, HARDY, KURONEKO; ASSISTANTS TO DR. LE FANU IN HIS EXPERIMENTS WITH VOLTAGE AND VOYEURISM.

THE BOUNTY-HUNTERS: ALTHOUGH A BRUTAL KILLER, CLETUS IS ALSO A RENOWNED ANIMAL –LOVER; LESTER PREFERS WOMEN.

PREACHER CARRION: CANDICE'S DADDY, HELLFIRE HEAD OF THE CHURCH OF THE NEW REVELATIONS OF BEING, IN WHICH AN ORGANLESS HUMAN ANATOMY FUSES WITH THE ROOT MATTER OF PROTOSTARS TO POSTULATE A GODLESS CONCEPT OF DIVINITY.

THE SAUSAGE-MAKER: AMOS DEMDYKE, MASTER BUTCHER AND ENGLAND'S MOST PROLIFIC SERIAL KILLER, WHO SWORE VENGEANCE ON ALL WOMEN AFTER HIS LEFT TESTICLE WAS BITTEN OFF AND DEVOURED BY A PROSTITUTE.

PANDORA: QUEEN OF THE CRIMSON NIGHT, MISTRESS OF THE "ZIPPER VIXENS" GIRL GANG, AND ONE OF THE SEVEN SOVEREIGNS WHO HOLD DOMINION OVER NOSFERATU NATION.

LEMUEL: PANDORA'S HUNCHBACKED SERVANT, AND CARCASS-KEEPER FOR THE ZIPPER VIXENS; HIS KIND WERE CLONED FROM AN ANCIENT INCUBUS SKULL.

THE SEVEN BRIDES OF BELPHEGOR: PANDORA'S PERSONAL BODYGUARD, BREEDERS OF FAMILIARS AND INSTIGATORS OF ORGIES.

SATURNALIA: QUEEN OF THE VELVET VOID, MISTRESS OF THE "CRUCIFIED CRAWLERS" GIRL GANG, AND ONE OF THE SEVEN SOVEREIGNS WHO HOLD DOMINION OVER NOSFERATU NATION.

LOCATIONS

CHATEAU DE SELLIGNY

THE SECLUDED MOUNTAIN RETREAT OF THE DUC DE BLANGIS, ONE OF THE RICHEST MEN – AND THE MOST NOTORIOUS LIBERTINE – IN THE WHOLE OF FRANCE. IN THE WINTER OF 1798, BLANGIS AND HIS THREE VICIOUS PARTNERS IN CRIME HELD A 120-DAY ORGY OF SEX, PERVERSION, RAPE, TORTURE, MUTILATION AND MURDER. OUTSIDE ON THE SNOW-COVERED HILLS, GANGS OF WOLVES ROAMED, RABID FROM EATING GUILLOTINED HUMAN MEAT. WHEN THE SURVIVORS OF THE ORGY LEFT SELLIGNY, THE WOLVES ATTACKED BY MOONLIGHT, DECAPITATING THE DOMINATRIX DESGRANGES AND WOUNDING SEVERAL OTHERS, INCLUDING BRISE-CUL, BLANGIS' FAVOURITE SODOMISER. AND SO THE CURSE OF SELLIGNY WAS BORNE BACK TO PARIS.

GHOST-CAT CASTLE

IN 1637, ON THE JAPANESE ISLAND OF AMAKUSA, THE SHOGUNS FAMOUSLY HARVESTED AND BURIED 11,111 SEVERED HEADS OF CHRISTIANS. 230 YEARS LATER SHURA, THE GREAT GREAT GRANDSON OF THE CHIEF EXECUTIONER WAS HIMSELF A BOY HEADSMAN TO THE LAST SHOGUN OF JAPAN. WHEN THE SAMURAI WERE OUTLAWED IN 1868, THIS LEGENDARY ASSASSIN FORMED A SECRET SECT OF RONIN ON THE ISLAND OF SADOGASHIMA.

IT WAS HERE THAT SHURA, NOW LORD OF GHOST-CAT CASTLE, TOOK CUSTODY OF HIS ORPHANED GRAND-DAUGHTER YUKI AFTER THE BOMBING OF HIROSHIMA, AND TRAINED HER IN THE OCCULT WAYS OF THE SAMURAI.

DEVIL'S DESERT

IN THE ABSENCE OF CIVILISATION, MEN ARE FREE – SOME SAY COMPELLED – TO REVERT TO THEIR PRIMAL NATURE. IN THE SHADOW OF THE SANTA SUSANA MOUNTAINS, RUMOURS ABOUND OF SATANIC CULTS: THE ORDER OF KIRKE, WHO KILL AND DRINK THE BLOOD OF DOGS; HELL'S ANGELS SECTS WHO FILM SNUFF MOVIES OF HUMAN SACRIFICES; AND ANOTHER BAND OF ACID-DAMAGED OUTLAWS WHOSE AIM IS TO PITCH BLACK AGAINST WHITE IN RACE RIOTS OF APOCALYPTIC VIOLENCE. LEGENDS ALSO TELL OF A GIRL SAMURAI WHO HAUNTS THE DUNES, BOTH HER PUSSY AND HER SWORD FOR SALE TO THE HIGHEST BIDDER, WHILST AT NIGHT THE CANYONS REVERBERATE WITH THE SCREAMS OF MEN RIPPED APART BY SHE-DEVILS.

HANGMAN'S HOVEL

IN THE DEAD HEART OF THE ATACHAFALAYA SWAMPLANDS, THE SHACK THAT FOR OVER A CENTURY HAS BEEN HOME TO BILLY TIMBERWOLF. STACKED ON A THOUSAND BONES OF THE BUTCHERED DEAD, IN THE SHADOW OF THE GALLOWS POLE. HERE, AT MIDNIGHT, SOME SAY YOU CAN HEAR BILLY PLAYING THE DEVIL'S MUSIC – "HELLHOUND ON MY TRAIL", "SMOKESTACK LIGHTNING", "ANGEL OF DEATH", "BABY LET'S PLAY HOUSE", "CRAWLING KING SNAKE", AND ALL THE OTHER FAVOURITES THAT REMIND HIM OF TWO CENTURIES OF REMORSELESS DEPREDATION. THIS IS ALSO WHERE SHAMANIC SHE-WOLF CARIL COVEN CHASES THE VOODOO DOWN.

PANDORA'S PUSSY PALACE

HOME OF THE "ZIPPER VIXENS", LOCATED IN LAS VEGAS, NEVADA. A LESBIAN WEDDING CHAPEL THAT DOUBLES AS AN ABATTOIR FOR PROCESSING MALE HUMAN CATTLE, WHOSE DRAINED BODY PARTS ARE STORED IN THE CRYPTS BENEATH WHILE HIGH PRIESTESS PANDORA PRESIDES OVER PSYCHEDELIC ORGIES.

PEACOCK PAGODA

HOME OF THE "99 BLOOD VIRGINS" GIRL GANG, LOCATED IN THE BORDER TOWN OF SANTA SANGRE, NEW MEXICO. HERE THE EYES OF MALE VICTIMS ARE HARVESTED AND USED IN ESOTERIC RITUALS OF SEX MAGICK WITH GOATS.

THE WHITE CAMELIA MENTAL INSTITUTE

FOUNDED BY DR. LAZARUS LE FANU IN LOUISIANA, FOR THE STUDY OF THE INSANE AND OTHER HUMAN ANOMALIES.

THE CHURCH: ONE OF FOUR MAIN INCARCERATION/OBSERVATION ZONES IN THE INSTITUTE, CREATED FOR THE STUDY OF INMATES SUFFERING FROM RELIGIOUS MANIA.

THE RING: CREATED FOR THE STUDY OF HOMICIDAL CIRCUS FREAKS, THE RING HAS A HISTORY OF CRUELTY AND VIOLENCE; IT WAS USED TO STAGE GLADIATORIAL BOUTS TO THE DEATH BY PRUVOST, THE INSTITUTE'S DEPUTY GOVERNOR.

THE KINO: A FILM-PROJECTION SPACE WHERE THE MOST HARDENED SERIAL KILLERS, SUCH AS AMOS DEMDYKE, ARE SHOWN REELS OF BOTH SIMULATED AND ACTUAL HUMAN CARNAGE AS AVERSION THERAPY.

THE KAMP: AN INCARCERATION ZONE FOR THE CRIMINALLY INSANE, A HIGH-SECURITY UNIT THAT HAS BEEN HOME TO SOME OF AMERICA'S MOST DANGEROUS INDIVIDUALS UNDERGOING ELECTRO-SHOCK TREATMENT.

THE CATACOMBS: A LABYRINTH THAT RUNS BENEATH THE INSTITUTE; AT ITS VERY CENTRE, RIGHT BELOW THE RING, IS A CIRCLE OF TOMBS THAT ARE BELIEVED TO HOUSE THE BODIES OF THE TWELVE GOLDEN KNIGHTS OF THE WHITE CAMELIA, THE ELITE OF THE ORGANIZATION WAITING FOR THEIR DAY OF RESURRECTION.

GRAVEYARD SEX (LUST FOR LIGHTNING)

THE CEMETERIES OF 19th CENTURY PARIS WERE RENOWNED AS THE HUNTING-GROUNDS OF THAT MOST NOTORIOUS OF SEXUAL ABBERANTS, THE NECROPHILE. AMONG THEM WERE SERGEANT BERTRAND AND VICTOR ARDISSON; LEGEND TELLS OF ANOTHER, EVEN MORE DERANGED FIGURE, A CANNIBAL WHO DEVOURED THE DEAD EVEN AS HE RAPED THEIR CORPSES, AND WHO WAS NEVER CAPTURED.

THIS SHADOWY FIGURE ALSO EMERGES IN TALES OF THE GRAVEYARDS OF RECONSTRUCTION-ERA NEW ORLEANS, WHERE DEPRAVED ARISTOCRATS WOULD MEET AT MIDNIGHT TO DRINK THE BLOOD OF PROSTITUTES UNDER THE SIGN OF THE WHITE CAMELIA. FOUNDED IN 1867, THE KNIGHTS OF THE WHITE CAMELIA WAS AN EARLY WHITE SUPREMACIST ORGANIZATION WHOSE RANKS INCLUDED THOSE FROM THE HIGHER STRATA OF SOCIETY. WITH UNDISCLOSED AFFILIATIONS TO THE KU KLUX KLAN, THE KNIGHTS WERE LARGELY DISBANDED WITHIN THREE YEARS, WITH SOME MEMBERS JOINING THE WHITE LEAGUE AND OTHER PARAMILITARY-STYLE GROUPS OF THE 1870s. LEGEND TELLS THAT THE KNIGHTS WILL RISE FROM THE DEAD WHENEVER AMERICA FACES THREAT FROM ADVERSARIES OF ETHNIC ORIGIN.

CEMETERIES ARE THE PERFECT PLACE FOR *GHOST-FUCKERS* – THOSE WHO SEEK SEXUAL COMMUNION WITH THE SOULS OF THE DEAD, AS OPPOSED TO THEIR MORTAL REMAINS. ONE SUCH WAS DIAMANDA COVEN, A WITCH OF THE WHITE VOODOO, WHO WOULD CRUELLY ABANDON HER DAUGHTER, CARIL, FOR MANY HOURS ON END WHILST HER SPIRIT REVELLED IN UNDERWORLD ORGIES. GHOST-FUCKERS WERE FERVENTLY HUNTED AND KILLED BY GROUPS OF RENEGADE LOUISIANA BAPTISTS KNOWN AS "SHELL-BOILERS".

EXCAVATED GRAVES LINED WITH BODY PARTS ARE, APPARENTLY, THE PERFECT CONJUGAL BED FOR THOSE WHO WOULD BE BRIDES OF THE THUNDERBOLT. A SOLITARY EYE-WITNESS ACCOUNT BEARS TESTAMENT TO THE PHENOMENON OF THE "LIGHTNING-FUCKERS": AT AROUND MIDNIGHT ON AUGUST 23, 1974, EULUPTUS KREEL, A TENNESSEE VAGRANT, CLAIMS TO HAVE SEEN A GANG OF TWO GIRLS AND ONE MALE DESECRATING A GRAVE DURING AN ELECTRICAL STORM; ONE OF THE GIRLS STRIPPED NAKED AND CLIMBED INTO THE HOLE FROM WHICH A ROTTING COFFIN HAD JUST BEEN HAULED, AND SOON AFTERWARDS A HUGE BOLT OF JAGGED LIGHTNING FLEW DOWN AND STRUCK HOME, ACCOMPANIED BY ORGASMIC MOANS AND SHRIEKS FROM THE GIRL AND LUNATIC HOWLING FROM HER COHORTS. AT THAT POINT KREEL, FEARING FOR HIS VERY LIFE, FLED THE SCENE. A POLICE INVESTIGATION THE FOLLOWING DAY REVEALED THE OPEN GRAVE, ITS SOIL NOW VITREFIED, HOUSING WHAT APPEARED TO BE THE CHARRED REMAINS OF A HUMAN UTERUS AND A SCATTERING OF DEADLY NIGHTSHADE.

THE SECLUDED MOUNTAIN RETREAT OF THE DUC DE BLANGIS, ONE OF THE RICHEST MEN – AND THE MOST NOTORIOUS LIBERTINE – IN THE WHOLE OF FRANCE. IN THE WINTER OF 1798, BLANGIS AND HIS THREE VICIOUS PARTNERS IN CRIME HELD A 120-DAY ORGY OF SEX, PERVERSION, RAPE, TORTURE, MUTILATION AND MURDER. OUTSIDE ON THE SNOW-COVERED HILLS, GANGS OF WOLVES ROAMED, RABID FROM EATING GUILLOTINED HUMAN MEAT.

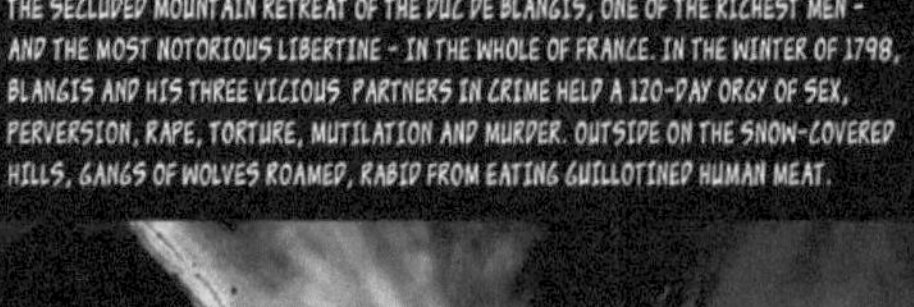

WHEN THE SURVIVORS OF THE ORGY LEFT SELLIGNY, THE WOLVES ATTACKED BY MOONLIGHT, DECAPITATING THE DOMINATRIX DESGRANGES AND WOUNDING SEVERAL OTHERS, INCLUDING BRISE-CUL, BLANGIS' FAVOURITE SODOMISER. AND SO THE CURSE OF SELLIGNY WAS BORNE BACK TO PARIS.

IN 1637, ON THE JAPANESE ISLAND OF AMAKUSA, THE SHOGUNS FAMOUSLY HARVESTED AND BURIED 11,111 SEVERED HEADS OF CHRISTIANS. 230 YEARS LATER SHURA, THE GREAT GREAT GRANDSON OF THE CHIEF EXECUTIONER WAS HIMSELF A BOY HEADSMAN TO THE LAST SHOGUN OF JAPAN. WHEN THE SAMURAI WERE OUTLAWED IN 1868, THIS LEGENDARY ASSASSIN FORMED A SECRET SECT OF *RONIN* ON THE ISLAND OF SADOGASHIMA.

IT WAS HERE THAT SHURA, NOW LORD OF GHOST-CAT CASTLE, TOOK CUSTODY OF HIS ORPHANED GRAND-DAUGHTER *YUKI* AFTER THE BOMBING OF HIROSHIMA, AND TRAINED HER IN THE OCCULT WAYS OF THE SAMURAI.

IN THE ABSENCE OF CIVILISATION, MEN ARE FREE – SOME SAY COMPELLED – TO REVERT TO THEIR PRIMAL NATURE. IN THE SHADOW OF THE SANTA SUSANA MOUNTAINS, RUMOURS ABOUND OF SATANIC CULTS: THE ORDER OF *KIRKE*, WHO KILL AND DRINK THE BLOOD OF DOGS; HELL'S ANGELS SECTS WHO FILM SNUFF MOVIES OF HUMAN SACRIFICES; AND ANOTHER BAND OF ACID-DAMAGED OUTLAWS WHOSE AIM IS TO PITCH BLACK AGAINST WHITE IN RACE RIOTS OF APOCALYPTIC VIOLENCE. LEGENDS ALSO TELL OF A GIRL SAMURAI WHO HAUNTS THE DUNES, BOTH HER PUSSY AND HER SWORD FOR SALE TO THE HIGHEST BIDDER, WHILST AT NIGHT THE CANYONS REVERBERATE WITH THE SCREAMS OF MEN RIPPED APART BY BLOOD-SUCKING SHE-DEVILS.

IN THE DEAD HEART OF THE ATCHAFALAYA SWAMPLANDS, THE SHACK THAT FOR OVER A CENTURY HAS BEEN HOME TO BILLY TIMBERWOLF. STACKED ON A THOUSAND BONES OF THE BUTCHERED DEAD, IN THE SHADOW OF THE GALLOWS POLE. HERE, AT MIDNIGHT, SOME SAY YOU CAN HEAR BILLY PLAYING THE DEVIL'S MUSIC – "HELLHOUND ON MY TRAIL", "SMOKESTACK LIGHTNING", "ANGEL OF DEATH", "BLUE MOON OF KENTUCKY", "CRAWLING KING SNAKE", AND ALL THE OTHER FAVOURITES THAT REMIND HIM OF TWO CENTURIES OF REMORSELESS DEPREDATION. THIS IS ALSO WHERE SHAMANIC SHE-WOLF CARIL COVEN CHASES THE VOODOO DOWN.

HOME OF THE "ZIPPER VIXENS", LOCATED IN LAS VEGAS, NEVADA. A LESBIAN WEDDING CHAPEL THAT DOUBLES AS AN ABATTOIR FOR PROCESSING MALE HUMAN CATTLE, WHOSE DRAINED BODY PARTS ARE STORED IN THE CRYPTS BENEATH WHILE HIGH PRIESTESS PANDORA PRESIDES OVER PEYOTE-FUELLED ORGIES.

HOME OF THE "99 BLOOD VIRGINS" GIRL GANG, LOCATED IN THE BORDER TOWN OF SANTA SANGRE, NEW MEXICO. HERE THE EYES OF MALE VICTIMS ARE HARVESTED AND USED IN ESOTERIC RITUALS OF SEX MAGICK WITH GOATS.

THE CHURCH: ONE OF FOUR MAIN INCARCERATION/OBSERVATION ZONES IN THE INSTITUTE, CREATED FOR THE STUDY OF INMATES SUFFERING FROM RELIGIOUS MANIA AND SATANIC DELUSIONS.

THE RING: CREATED FOR THE STUDY OF HOMICIDAL CIRCUS FREAKS, THE RING HAS A HISTORY OF CRUELTY AND VIOLENCE; IT WAS USED TO STAGE GLADIATORIAL BOUTS TO THE DEATH BY PRUVOST, THE INSTITUTE'S DEPUTY GOVERNOR.

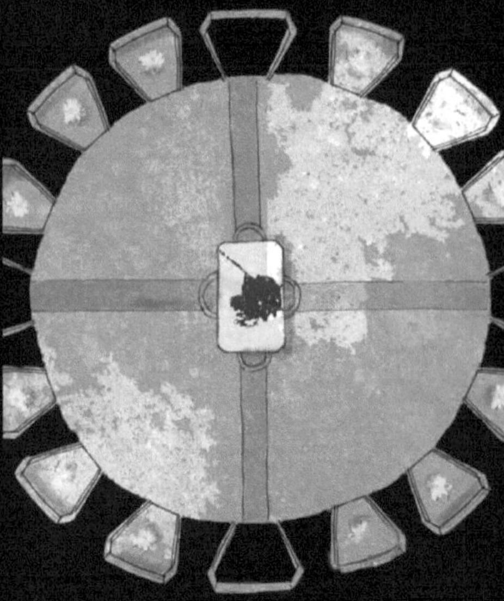

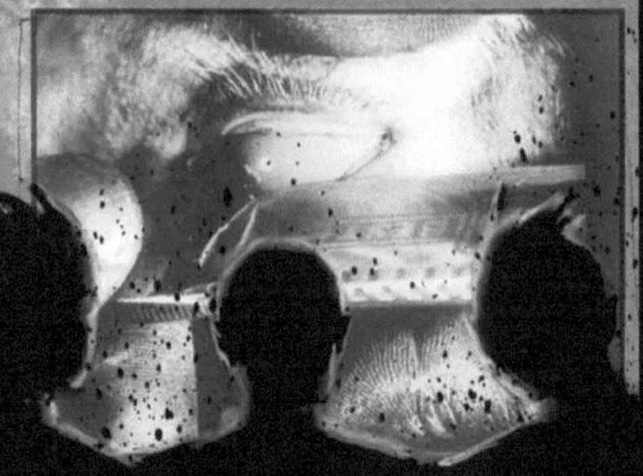

THE KINO: A FILM-PROJECTION SPACE WHERE THE MOST PSYCHOPATHIC SERIAL KILLERS, SUCH AS AMOS DEMDYKE, ARE SHOWN REELS OF BOTH SIMULATED AND ACTUAL HARDCORE HUMAN CARNAGE AND ATROCITY AS AVERSION THERAPY.

THE MAZE: A CATACOMBS THAT RUNS BENEATH THE INSTITUTE; AT ITS VERY CENTRE, RIGHT BELOW THE RING, IS A CIRCLE OF TOMBS THAT ARE BELIEVED TO HOUSE THE BODIES OF THE TWELVE GOLDEN KNIGHTS OF THE WHITE CAMELIA, THE ELITE OF THE ORGANIZATION WAITING FOR THEIR DAY OF RESURRECTION.

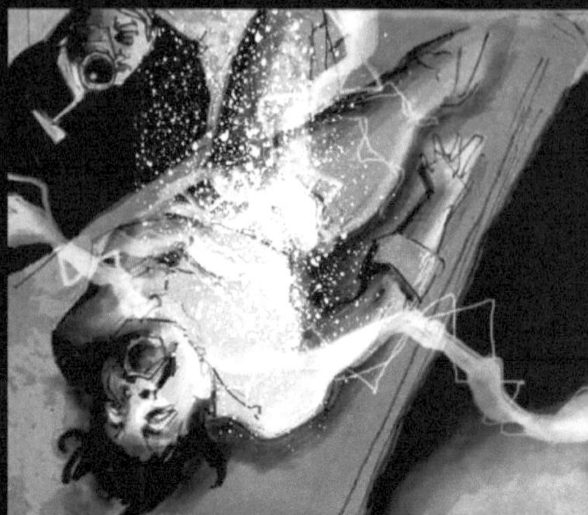

THE KAMP: A HIGH-SECURITY PENAL UNIT THAT HAS BEEN HOME TO SOME OF AMERICA'S MOST DANGEROUS INDIVIDUALS UNDERGOING RADICAL ELECTRO-SHOCK TREATMENT AND OTHER COVERT EXPERIMENTATION.

THE CEMETERIES OF 19TH CENTURY PARIS WERE RENOWNED AS THE HUNTING-GROUNDS OF THAT MOST NOTORIOUS OF SEXUAL ABBERANTS, THE *NECROPHILE*. AMONG THEM WERE SERGEANT BERTRAND AND VICTOR ARDISSON; LEGEND TELLS OF ANOTHER, EVEN MORE DERANGED FIGURE, A CANNIBAL WHO DEVOURED THE DEAD EVEN AS HE RAPED THEIR CORPSES, AND WHO WAS NEVER CAPTURED.

THIS SHADOWY FIGURE ALSO EMERGES IN TALES OF THE GRAVEYARDS OF RECONSTRUCTION-ERA NEW ORLEANS, WHERE DEPRAVED ARISTOCRATS WOULD MEET AT MIDNIGHT TO DRINK THE BLOOD OF PROSTITUTES UNDER THE SIGN OF THE FLOWER OF FLESH. FOUNDED IN 1867, THE *KNIGHTS OF THE WHITE CAMELIA* WAS AN EARLY WHITE SUPREMACIST ORGANIZATION WHOSE RANKS INCLUDED THOSE FROM THE HIGHER STRATA OF SOCIETY. WITH UNDISCLOSED AFFILIATIONS TO THE *KU KLUX KLAN*, THE KNIGHTS WERE LARGELY DISBANDED WITHIN THREE YEARS, WITH SOME MEMBERS JOINING THE WHITE LEAGUE AND OTHER PARAMILITARY-STYLE GROUPS OF THE 1870S. LEGEND TELLS THAT THE KNIGHTS WILL RISE FROM THE DEAD WHENEVER AMERICA FACES THREAT FROM ADVERSARIES OF ETHNIC ORIGIN.

CEMETERIES ARE THE PERFECT PLACE FOR *GHOST-FUCKERS* - THOSE WHO SEEK SEXUAL COMMUNION WITH THE SOULS OF THE DEAD, AS OPPOSED TO THEIR MORTAL REMAINS. ONE SUCH WAS DIAMANDA COVEN, A WITCH OF THE WHITE VOODOO, WHO WOULD CRUELLY ABANDON HER DAUGHTER, *CARIL*, FOR MANY HOURS ON END WHILST HER SPIRIT REVELLED IN UNDERWORLD ORGIES. GHOST-FUCKERS WERE FERVENTLY HUNTED AND KILLED BY GROUPS OF RENEGADE LOUISIANA BAPTISTS KNOWN AS "SHELL-BOILERS".

EXCAVATED GRAVES LINED WITH BODY PARTS ARE THE PERFECT CONJUGAL BED FOR THOSE WHO WOULD BE BRIDES OF THE THUNDERBOLT. A SOLITARY EYE-WITNESS ACCOUNT BEARS TESTAMENT TO THE PHENOMENON OF THE "LIGHTNING-FUCKERS": AT AROUND MIDNIGHT ON AUGUST 23, 1974, EULUPTUS KREEL, A TENNESSEE VAGRANT, CLAIMS TO HAVE SEEN A GANG OF TWO GIRLS AND ONE MALE DESECRATING A GRAVE DURING AN ELECTRICAL STORM; ONE OF THE GIRLS STRIPPED NAKED AND CLIMBED INTO THE HOLE FROM WHICH A ROTTING COFFIN HAD JUST BEEN HAULED, AND SOON AFTERWARDS A HUGE BOLT OF JAGGED LIGHTNING FLEW DOWN AND STRUCK HOME, ACCOMPANIED BY ORGASMIC MOANS AND SHRIEKS FROM THE GIRL AND LUNATIC HOWLING FROM HER COHORTS. AT THAT POINT KREEL, FEARING FOR HIS VERY LIFE, FLED THE SCENE. A POLICE INVESTIGATION THE FOLLOWING DAY REVEALED THE OPEN GRAVE, ITS SOIL NOW VITREFIED, HOUSING WHAT APPEARED TO BE THE CHARRED REMAINS OF A HUMAN UTERUS AND A SCATTERING OF DEADLY NIGHTSHADE.

LUST FOR LIGHTNING

PROLOGUE

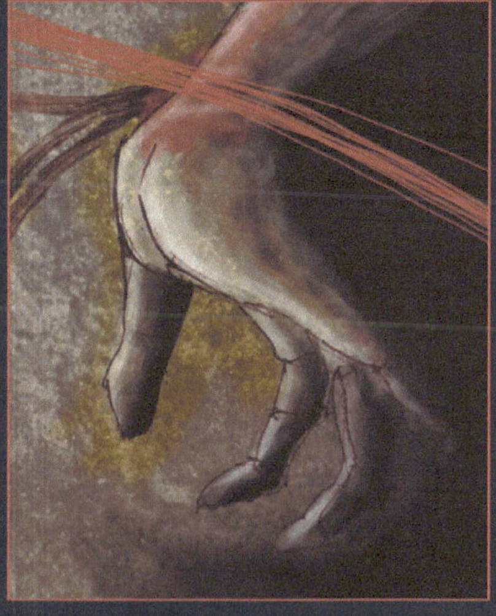

IN AND OUT OF FLESH

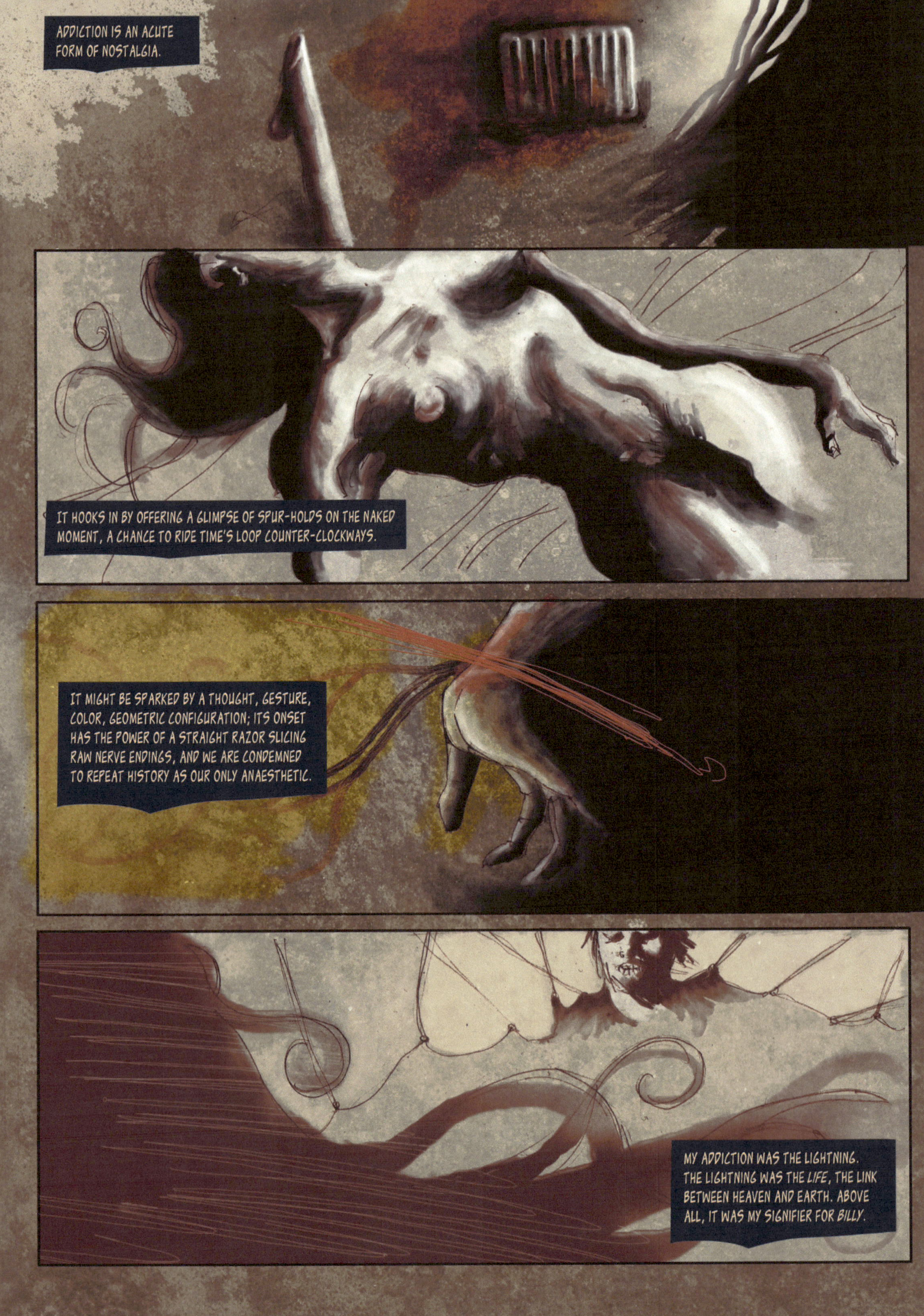

ADDICTION IS AN ACUTE FORM OF NOSTALGIA.
IT HOOKS IN BY OFFERING A GLIMPSE OF SPUR-HOLDS ON THE NAKED MOMENT, A CHANCE TO RIDE TIME'S LOOP COUNTER-CLOCKWAYS.
IT MIGHT BE SPARKED BY A THOUGHT, GESTURE, COLOR, GEOMETRIC CONFIGURATION; ITS ONSET HAS THE POWER OF A STRAIGHT RAZOR SLICING RAW NERVE ENDINGS, AND WE ARE CONDEMNED TO REPEAT HISTORY AS OUR ONLY ANAESTHETIC.
MY ADDICTION WAS THE LIGHTNING. THE LIGHTNING WAS THE LIFE, THE LINK BETWEEN HEAVEN AND EARTH. ABOVE ALL, IT WAS MY SIGNIFIER FOR BILLY.

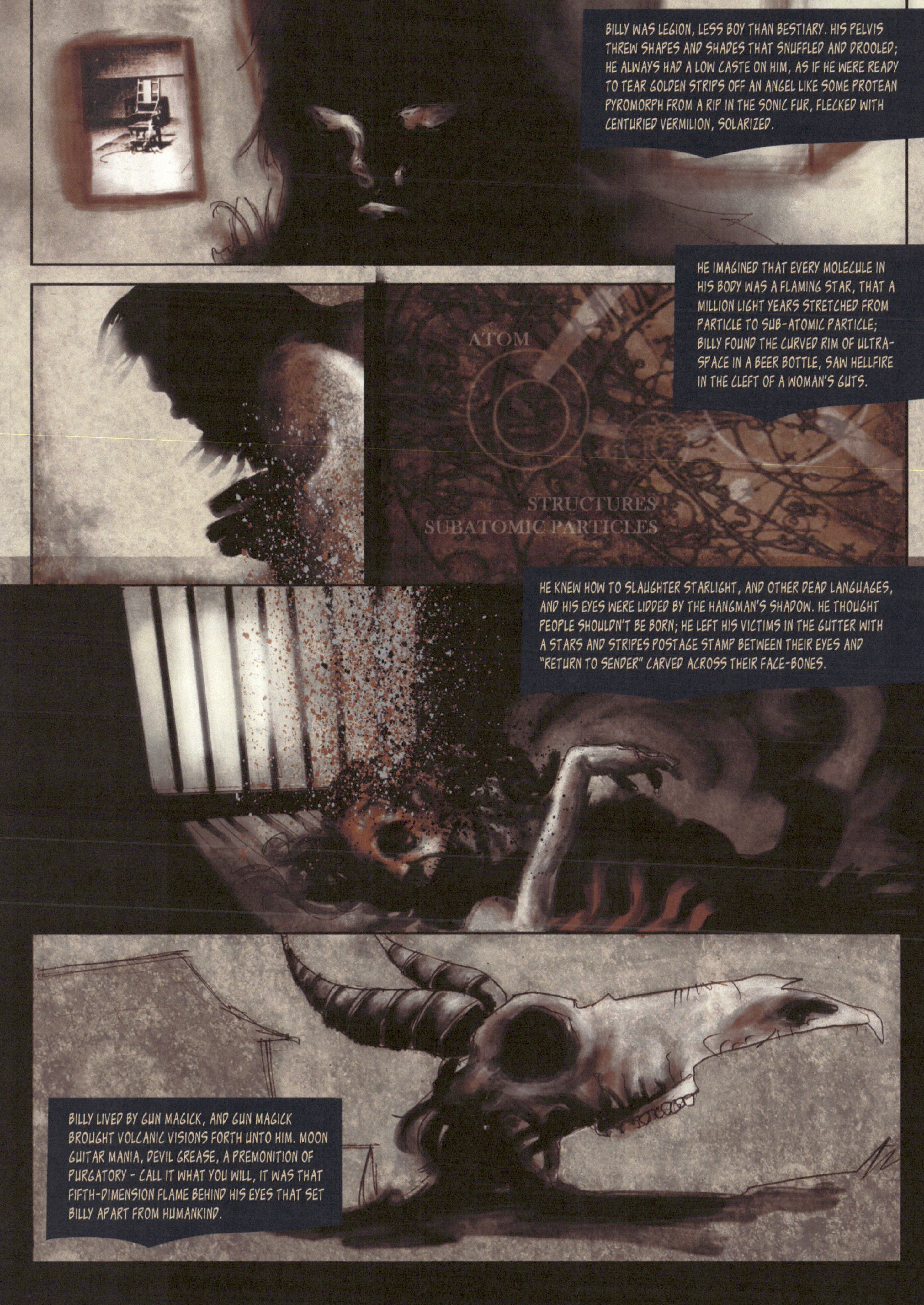

BILLY WAS LEGION, LESS BOY THAN BESTIARY. HIS PELVIS THREW SHAPES AND SHADES THAT SNUFFLED AND DROOLED; HE ALWAYS HAD A LOW CASTE ON HIM, AS IF HE WERE READY TO TEAR GOLDEN STRIPS OFF AN ANGEL LIKE SOME PROTEAN PYROMORPH FROM A RIP IN THE SONIC FUR, FLECKED WITH CENTURIED VERMILION, SOLARIZED.
HE IMAGINED THAT EVERY MOLECULE IN HIS BODY WAS A FLAMING STAR, THAT A MILLION LIGHT YEARS STRETCHED FROM PARTICLE TO SUB-ATOMIC PARTICLE; BILLY FOUND THE CURVED RIM OF ULTRA-SPACE IN A BEER BOTTLE, SAW HELLFIRE IN THE CLEFT OF A WOMAN'S GUTS.
ATOM
STRUCTURES
SUBATOMIC PARTICLES
HE KNEW HOW TO SLAUGHTER STARLIGHT, AND OTHER DEAD LANGUAGES, AND HIS EYES WERE LIDDED BY THE HANGMAN'S SHADOW. HE THOUGHT PEOPLE SHOULDN'T BE BORN; HE LEFT HIS VICTIMS IN THE GUTTER WITH A STARS AND STRIPES POSTAGE STAMP BETWEEN THEIR EYES AND "RETURN TO SENDER" CARVED ACROSS THEIR FACE-BONES.
BILLY LIVED BY GUN MAGICK, AND GUN MAGICK BROUGHT VOLCANIC VISIONS FORTH UNTO HIM. MOON GUITAR MANIA, DEVIL GREASE, A PREMONITION OF PURGATORY - CALL IT WHAT YOU WILL, IT WAS THAT FIFTH-DIMENSION FLAME BEHIND HIS EYES THAT SET BILLY APART FROM HUMANKIND.

BILLY'S ONE AND TRUE GIRLFRIEND, CARIL, CALLED HERSELF FIRESKIN. BILLY BIT HER SOFT AND DEEP ONE PURE WHITE NIGHT, THE VENOM OF THE BEAST IN HIS SPIT LIKE ANCIENT RABIES FROM THE SLABS.
HER HAIR WAS RED LIKE HARD SUGAR ON A HEXAGRAM OF ROTTEN JACKDAWS, AND THEY HELD HANDS WITH LIGHTNING CHAINS AT MIDNIGHT. THEIR YELPS WERE HEARD IN CEMETERIES.
PLEDGING ALLEGIANCE TO A RAVEN SUN, BILLY AND CARIL CLEAVED TIGHT TO THE DARK SIDE OF THE ROAD. THE MUSIC ON THE RADIO HOWLED LIKE A HOMICIDE: PROCLAMATIONS IN BLACK, A CROSS-CUT SAW, AND THE CLICKING OF OLD DRY BONES IN A PASSWAY.

THEY PICKED UP YUKI HITCHING IN DEVILS CANYON. SHE SEEMED TO BE MADE OUT OF NEON, A SILVER REBOP FOR THE BUZZARDS; SHE ONLY BECAME TRULY VISIBLE BY NIGHT.
ONCE YUKI WAS BIT, SHE DREAMED OF DOGSTARS, DITCHES AND BLOSSOMING JUGULAR WOUNDS. HER AND CARIL SOON BECAME LIKE SISTERS, HAUNTERS OF THE SOFT WHITE UNDERBELLY; THEY TOOK TO KEEPING EACH OTHER'S MENSTRUAL BLOOD IN BOTTLES, AS KEEPSAKES AND ALSO AS A KIND OF PSYCHO-ACID TO THROW IN THE SICK FACES OF MEN.

BILLY'S GANG WAS TUNED IN TO A FEEDING-GROUND OF THE MARAUDING DEAD, A LIMBO LARDER STUFFED FULL OF STOLEN SKIN, ENTRAILS, MEAT AND BONES THAT COULD REPLACE WHAT THE LIGHTNING BURNT OUT. THEY STALKED THIS REGURGITATED GRAIL WITH THE TENACITY OF A HEAT-SEEKING PATHOGEN, A CAUSTIC CONTAGION CLOSING IN.

THEIR AXIS WAS AS TUMID AND PROFANE AS A BEAUTY PROCESSION OF BOWEL-WORMS IN A DESECRATED CONVENT, THEIR TRANSPORTS LAVED IN LUNAR BLOODSTORMS.

THEY WERE THE FEW, THE ONES BORN WITH A PAW-PRINT ON THE SOUL.

THEY WERE THE TEENAGE TIMBERWOLVES.

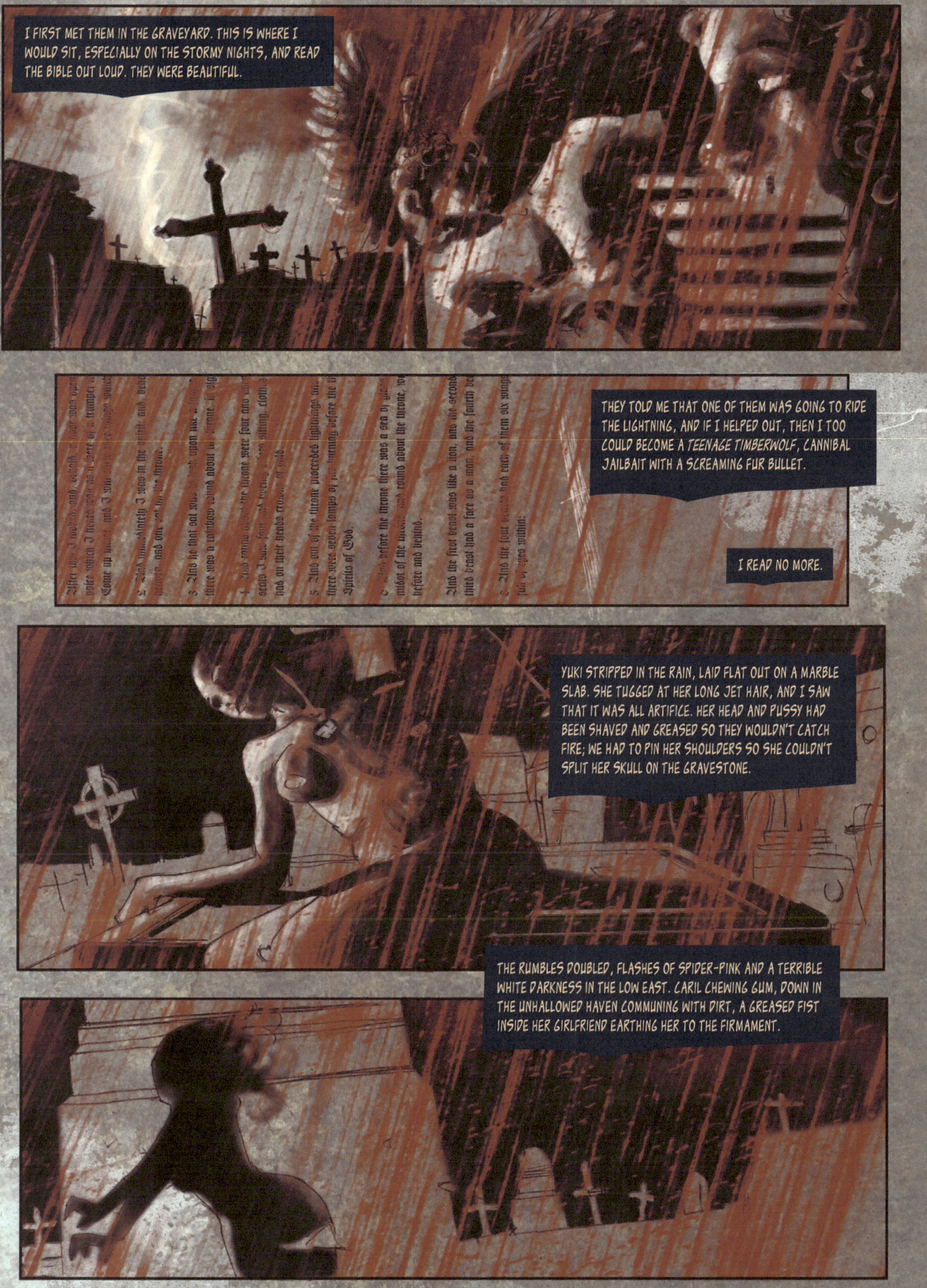

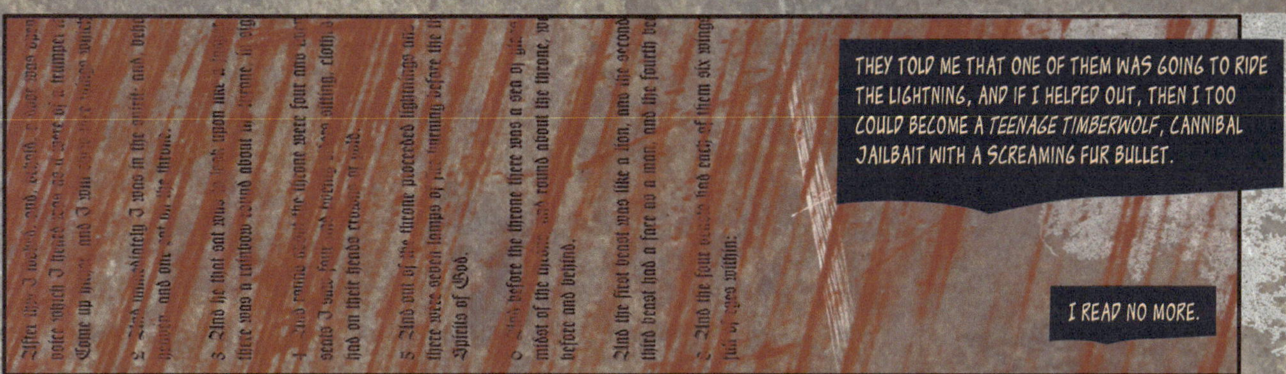

YUKI STRIPPED IN THE RAIN, LAID FLAT OUT ON A MARBLE SLAB. SHE TUGGED AT HER LONG JET HAIR, AND I SAW THAT IT WAS ALL ARTIFICE. HER HEAD AND PUSSY HAD BEEN SHAVED AND GREASED SO THEY WOULDN'T CATCH FIRE; WE HAD TO PIN HER SHOULDERS SO SHE COULDN'T SPLIT HER SKULL ON THE GRAVESTONE.

THE RUMBLES DOUBLED, FLASHES OF SPIDER-PINK AND A TERRIBLE WHITE DARKNESS IN THE LOW EAST. CARIL CHEWING GUM, DOWN IN THE UNHALLOWED HAVEN COMMUNING WITH DIRT, A GREASED FIST INSIDE HER GIRLFRIEND EARTHING HER TO THE FIRMAMENT.

THE BOLT STRUCK, DIFFUSING ITS POWER THROUGH YUKI'S CONVULSING BODY. I FELT THE COSMIC CRASH IN MY OWN CLENCHED FINGERS, SAW IT SURGE DOWN HER ARMS IN COLD BLUE, RAISE GLYPHS ACROSS HER RIB-CAGE, BELLY TAUT WITH ELECTRIC STRIATIONS, LEGS JERKING WIDE APART, TURNED HER CLEAN OVER, POISON IVY ABLAZE, THE FUCKING STONE NEARLY SPLIT IN HALF, HER TITS NOW BUZZING LIKE GENERATORS, SPARKS AND STEAMING PISS SHOT BACK INTO THE BONEYARD BLACKNESS.
BILLY MOUNTED HER, CYCLE BOOTS ON CARIL'S SHOULDERS, HER EYES STELLAR, CIRCLING EACH THUMB AND FOREFINGER INTO HIS MOUTH, WITHDREW THEM DRIPPING SPIT AND REACHED ROUND TO ENGAGE YUKI'S NIPPLES.
A SHARP CRACK AND HIS FOREARMS JOLTED, SMELL OF SINGED SCAR TISSUE; A LATTICE OF BLUE LIGHT SPURTED FROM HIS FINGERTIPS, UP THROUGH HIS ARMS TO HIS SHOULDERS AS IF EMBALMED ALIVE BY RADIOACTIVE COBALT, BONES VISIBLE IN GLACIAL ORGASM.

I HELPED PEEL YUKI FROM THE SLAB, SMOKE-BREATHING, LEAVING BEHIND GREAT SHEETS OF CHARRED SKIN. CARIL TALKING OF NIGHTSHADE AND NEPENTHE, SOULS SPITTED ON LIGATURES OF BROILING DOG-BONE. WE WERE IMMERSED, AS IF THE TWILIGHT'S GIZZARD HAD CHOKED OVER, STRANDING US IN THE GUT TRACT OF SOME MUMMIFIED SNAKE; THE WORDS IN MY BRAIN WERE HOOK-SHAPED, SCORPIONS WRITHING UNDER THEIR THIN MEMBRANE, STRAINING TO FIND LIGHT. WE HAD SOAKED UP EVERY GLIMPSE.
IN THE DAYS AND NIGHTS THAT FOLLOWED, WE LIVED IN CRYPTS. BILLY SAID THAT IN THE TIME AFTER A STORM, IT WAS BEST TO SLEEP WITH DEAD SKULLS, RECEPTACLES FOR THE DARKEST MERCIES OF THE DEW. AND SO THEY LANGUISHED, SEEM AS LIKE POISED BETWEEN LIFE AND DEATH. THEIR ENERVATION WAS THAT OF THE DAMNED. I DECIDED THAT THEY WERE TRUE PROMETHEAN LEPERS, UPHOLDERS OF A BEAUTY TOO PURE FOR THIS EXTINGUISHED WORLD. A BEAUTY CAGED IN BRIMSTONE, FRAMED BY BAROQUE OBSIDIAN CURVATURES THAT ARCED INTO A FRACTAL INFINITY OF FANGS.

CARIL'S MAMA WAS A WHITE TRASH, *GRIS-GRIS* GHOST-FUCKER GIFTED WITH THE *SEVENTH SIGHT*; HER NIGHTLY SOJOURNS IN THE UNDERWORLD WERE APOPLEXIES OF SEX WITH DEAD SOULS. WHEN HER VACANT BODY WAS FOUND AND BOILED ALIVE BY BAPTISTS, HER DISCORPORATED SPIRIT COULD ONLY FIND REFUGE INSIDE CARIL'S SAWDUST, STITCH-MOUTH DOLL, *DELILAH*.

NOW CARIL TOOK TO TRANCES, TRIPS INSIDE TRANSFIGURED TIME WHERE FIRE-WALKERS SPOKE TO HER FROM VOODOO PALISADES.

HE LIKENED MY YELLOW HAIR TO LEOPARDSKINS AND LUREX. HE SAID THAT I WAS A TRUE HARBINGER OF INSECT PANIC, THE KEEPER OF THE VANILLA VAULT, A BLONDE WITCH SO FULL OF BLONDE MAGICK THAT IT WAS SOAKING THROUGH THE CROTCH OF MY PANTIES. HE RECKONED I HAD FALLEN ANGELS ON MY MIND. PROBABLY KEPT PUPPY-DOGS' EYEBALLS STASHED IN A PUZZLE-BOX, ORCHIDS IN A CONCRETE CLAW. I WAS FOURTEEN YEARS OLD.

WHEN IT WAS TIME TO LEAVE, I WENT WITH THEM GLADLY, BUT I WAS NOT ALLOWED TO TOUCH BILLY. THIS BURNED MY SOUL.

OUTSIDE STORM SEASON, WE SHIFTED IN HOT SHADOW. WAY INTO THE DESERT, PAST A GALLOWS TURNPIKE, WE CAME TO A PLACE WHERE THE SOIL WAS DUST-RED AND UNREPENTANT. BILLY KNEW THAT A MAN HAD TO SUFFER BEFORE HE DESERVED THE HARBOUR OF THE DITCH; ANYTHING LESS AND THAT SOIL WOULD SPIT BACK YOUR UNRIPE BONES LIKE WATERMELON SEEDS. BILLY LIKED THAT TERRAIN; THERE WERE THINGS IN THE FOOTHILLS WHICH MOVED, CASTING SHADOWS THAT RESEMBLED DUNG POURING FROM AN ANUS.
HE SWORE TO IMPRINT THE DUNES WITH A LIVID CICATRIX OF HIS OWN DEVICES, A WEB FROM WHICH WOULD DANGLE THE HIDES OF THE RIGHTEOUS ON THE BREEZE, WHILE HE SLIPPED, WANTON, IN AND OUT OF FLESH, FROM EXISTENCE TO ETHER AND BACK AGAIN.
WE WERE SKIN-STEALERS, LIGHTNING-FUCKERS, OUR CADAVER CRUISE WAS TILTED AT THE CLOACA. BILLY SAID WE WERE PROPHETS OF A MESENTERIC INTERLUDE BETWEEN MAN AND WOLF; OUR VERY PISS WAS HARD RAIN, FOAMING SNAKE JETSAM LEVELLED AT THE HEARTS OF THE INIQUITOUS. OUR BODIES STANK AND CRAWLED WITH LICE, BUT OUR SOULS WOULD BE ENTHRONED IN HOLY LAIRS PAVED WITH OFFAL, FURNISHED WITH FEMURS, WALLED BY ENDLESS SLABS OF BLOODY HUMAN MEAT.

RETURN
TO SENDER
WE BURIED HEADS WHERE THE MOON FELL.

CHAPTER ONE

BIBLE BURNER

MY NAME IS CANDICE, BY THE WAY.
MY MAMA DIED IN CHILDBIRTH AND I WAS RAISED BY MY DADDY, A HELLFIRE SNAKE-HANDLER, IN SUGARTOWN, ALABAMA.
BROADSIDES FROM A BARBED WIRE PULPIT, SUNGLASSES AFTER DARK. BLAZING BIBLES ON THE CUSP OF WHIPCORD, IN THE SOFT DIVIDE BETWEEN A RATTLESNAKE TWIST AND THE THUNDERBOLT KISS OF VENGEANCE.
YEAH.
WELCOME TO THE CHURCH OF THE NEW REVELATIONS OF BEING.

CANDY, TAKE THIS BUCKET OF SHIT AND PLACE IT BY YOUR MAMA'S GRAVE.
THE SHIT IS SWEET, THE MOON IS BRIGHT AND THIRSTY. INFERNAL LAVA FUNNELS BELOW, COILING BONES INTO BLONDE FIRE.
YOU BEAR THE SLIT BETWEEN YOUR LEGS. IT IS THE NIGHT OF THE RAVEN.
MAMA, CAN YOU HEAR ME?
WHEN THE STORM BREAKS, THE SHIT WILL BOIL, THE TARANTULAS WILL LAY THEIR BLACK EGGS INSIDE YOUR SKULL.
THE STORM IS MADE OF ROSES AND IT NEVER SNOWS IN SUGARTOWN.
DADDY SAYS THAT THE NEW FLESH WILL ABSTAIN FROM MATTER TO FULMINATE IN THE VOID OF VIOLENCE, ETERNALLY AND WITHOUT RECOURSE TO SEMBLANCE OF INTERNAL ILLUMINATION. HE CALLS THIS THE RODEZ PRINCIPLE.

"A SLENDER BELLY. A BELLY OF FINE POWDER, LIKE A PICTURE. AN EXPLODED GRENADE AT THE BASE OF THE BELLY. THE GRENADE CASTS A FLEECY CIRCULATION, RISING LIKE TONGUES OF FIRE, COLD FIRE. THE CIRCULATION CATCHES THE BELLY, TURNS IT OVER. ONLY THE BELLY WILL NOT TURN. THE VEINS ARE FULL OF HEADY BLOOD, BLOOD MIXED WITH SAFFRON AND SULPHUR, ONLY SULPHUR SWEETENED WITH WATER..."

"...BREASTS APPEAR ABOVE THE BELLY. HIGHER STILL, AND IN DEPTH, BUT ON ANOTHER LEVEL OF THE MIND, THE SUN AFLAME, ONLY IN SUCH A WAY AS TO MAKE US THINK THE BREAST IS BURNING. AND AT THE BASE OF THE GRENADE, A BIRD."

AND SO, MONTHLY BY MOONSHINE, I WOULD DELIVER DADDY'S DEVOTION TO MAMA. SOMETIMES I WOULD SEE SCAVENGER DOGS FUCKING AMONG THE TOMBSTONES, AND FEEL IT SHARP IN MY PUSSY. BLOOD, SHIT, HEAT, BLUE LIGHT, A FERAL EYE OF FLOWERS PULSING IN THAT NOCTURNAL ARCADE OF EVISCERATED WRAITHS AND MARTYRS.

AS I WAITED, UNKNOWINGLY, FOR BILLY.

CHAPTER TWO

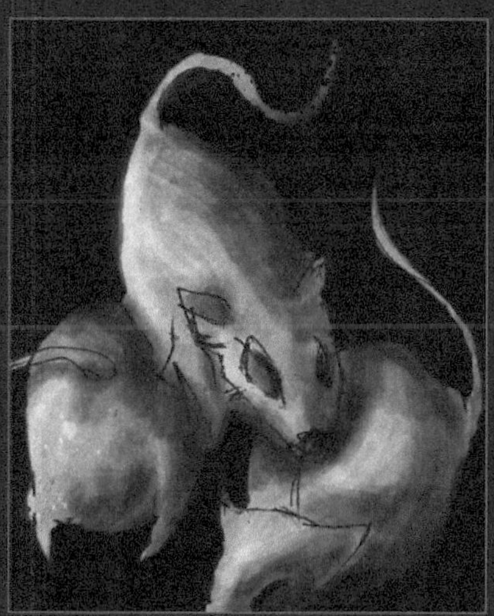

BLOOD-TRIP ON HELLCAT HIGHWAY

LAS VEGAS.

IT REMINDS ME OF HOME, OF HIROSHIMA. PREDATION, COPULATION, ASSASSINATION, SOLAR TYRANNY PILED ON A BEDROCK OF VITREFIED SAND. THEY SAID THE CITY FIREBALLED AS THE CANCER ATE THROUGH MY MOTHER'S CERVIX, THE SLAP OF HER WOMB ON THE SLOP TRAY ECHOING THE OPEN FIST THAT BLASTED FROM MY LUNGS THE FIRST SCREAM OF HATE AND PAIN, ITSELF A SONIC FOREBEAR OF THE LAMENTATIONS OF THE SKINLESS. WHILE MY FATHER WRITHES BLIND AND BEREFT OF LIMBS AND THE BLACK RAIN CONFIGURES A VORTEX OF ACID IN THE PRIMAL PLACENTA.

I WAS BORN TO BURN.

ELECTRIC LADY LOUNGE

I NEED A FUCKING DRINK.

THIS WORLD IS A HIDEOUS, OVERLIT PLACE, EVERYWHERE THE INTERSTICES OF AN INVIOLABLE MIRROR BEHIND WHICH LIES A TERRIBLE ZOMBIE ZONE, HAUNTED BY BILLY TIMBERWOLF AND THE GHOSTS OF ELECTRICITY. I WALK ON A FLUX OF FULGURITES, A BURNT-OUT HIGHWAY STAR SLIPPING LIKE TRASH THROUGH SUMMER'S ROTTING FINGERS, BEGGING FOR THE FORKED FIST OF JESUS TO FUCK ME DEAD. WHY DOES BILLY ALWAYS SEND ME TO FETCH HIS BEER AND BONES?

BOY-FOOD, NAKED SAND, ANGELS BLAZE BY NIGHT. THE MOON IS SILVER AND IT WEEPS FOR US.
WE DRINK THE CUM, THE PISS, THE BLOOD; THE MEAT AND BONES ARE KEPT ON ICE. WHEN SKULLS HANG IN MALIGNANT MIRRORS, BELLADONNA BLISTERS BLACK, THE SWITCHBLADE GLITTERS THIRTEEN TIMES. DO YOU LIKE MY NECKLACE?
TINY JAPANESE COCKS. FUCKING SHIT.
I HAVE ONE JUST LIKE IT.
HOW ABOUT THAT MEAT?
TONIGHT, IT'S OFF THE BONE.
THE BITCH SMELLS LIKE A CORPSE, BUT COLD, NOT FRESH ENOUGH TO EAT. PAST A SPINE OF CAVES WHERE DESERT BATS ROOST AND SCORPIONS WHEEL, MOVING AWAY FROM THE CITY, AWAY FROM THE GRAVEYARD WHERE BILLY'S WAITING FOR ME. BUT THE NIGHT IS SPECTRAL, IT SHOWERS THE DUNES WITH A DELUGE OF COSMIC ECTOPLASM, LIQUID DUST FROM A SWASTIKA OF STARS. I CAN SEE FIRE. I CAN HEAR SCREAMS. I CAN SMELL BLOOD.
PIG-STABBING TIME.

VAMPIRE VEIN-SHREDDERS IN DUNE BUGGIES. CRUISING THE NIGHT, PREYING ON COUPLES; THE MALES CRUCIFIED, DRAINED OF THEIR JUICES, CONSUMED BY THE FLAMES OR BURIED NECK-DEEP IN THE SAND, BUTTERED HEADS BESET BY FIRE-ANTS. BUT WHAT ABOUT THE FEMALES?
VISIONS OF REVOLVING SKY-FIRE, THE SMELL OF SPILT FAECES, THE CLACK OF RAW PELVIS UNDER A GUN BARREL, THE SILKY TWITCH OF OFFAL AS IT HATCHES. THE IRON IN MY CUNT-BLOOD IS IMPRINTED WITH TRACE FROM FIRST GENERATION PLANETS, EACH CELL ENCODED WITH THE REFLEX TO DESTROY WORLDS.
TONIGHT I'LL LEAD BILLY TO THE SHE-BUTCHERS' CRYPT.

PLEASE DON'T EAT US...
I'LL TAKE THIS HOME TO MY DADDY...
...THE BIG BAD WOLF.
BUT THE MOON VEERS TO VENUS, OUR PISS BOILS WITH PEYOTE, NEW GIRL FLESH FLOWERS FOR THE BLACK LEATHER BRIDES. THIS IS THE HOUR OF THE THIRD EYE BUTTERFLY.
COME AND MEET OUR MOMMY...
...THE PUSSY QUEEN OF THE NIGHT.
AND SO WE WAITED. BILLY DREAMING OF COLD BEER AND BABY-FAT, CARIL OF HER DEMON SISTER. OUR EYES LIKE SORROWING SCARS ON A SPIDER'S WEB.
SCORPIO DRIVES A BLACK CADILLAC TO HELL.
"THERE IS AN ACID, TURBID ANGUISH, AS SHARP AS A KNIFE, WHOSE QUARTERINGS WEIGH THE EARTH, FLASHING ANGUISH, PUNCTUATED BY ABYSMS, SQUASHED AND SQUEEZED LIKE BUGS, LIKE A SORT OF HARDENED VERMIN, ALL MOVEMENT FROZEN..."
"...EXTREME COLD. AGONIZING ABSTINENCE. BONE AND SINEW NIGHTMARE LIMBO, A SENSATION OF GASTRIC FUNCTIONS FLAPPING LIKE A FLAG IN THE CORPOSANT OF THE STORM..."
"...A SHATTERING ARBORESCENCE AND THREADBARE, SHINY BROWS REFLECTED, WITH SOMETHING LIKE A PERFECT NAVEL, BUT INDISTINCT, THE COLOUR OF BLOOD DILUTED WITH WATER, AND IN FRONT OF IT, A GRENADE WHICH ALSO SHED BLOOD MIXED WITH WATER, WHICH SCATTERED BLOOD WITH LINES DRIPPING DOWN. AND IN THESE LINES, BREAST-CIRCLES DRAWN IN THE BRAIN'S BLOOD."

YUKI MUST'VE PICKED UP A JOHN. I WARNED HER NOT TO... NOT IN THE CITY. THE CITY IS A ROCKET FROM THE TOMBS - THE HIGHWAY IS FOR HELLCATS.
LOOKING FOR LIGHTNING, DOWN BY LAW.
SHE PROBABLY JUST WENT FOR A STEAK...
Pandora's Pussy Palace
WELCOME TO THE CHAPEL OF LOVE.
THIS MUST BE IT - THE SKIN CITY BLOODGATES. INSIDE, THE MEAT, BONES AND GUTS; ENOUGH TO FEED US FOR CENTURIES. FIRST, LET'S SEE HOW THESE BITCHES LIKE TO PLAY.

FOAMING PISS IN GOBLETS, A GAUD OF DRIPPING ROSES. FANG PUNCTURES CLIT, SNAP OF SILVER RING, CHAINS CRISS-CROSS IN MUSK OF METALLIC GLAMOUR. LET IT BLEED, LET IT SCREAM.
A TIGERSKIN TRAUMA DISSOLVING INTO ANAMORPHIC GLOBULES, ALL NERVE-ENDINGS SOLARIZED IN A STROBIC OCCLUSION OF THE VISUAL CORTEX.
SLIT-DRINKERS LICK MY EYEBALLS IN PERPETUAL IRIDESCENT SPIRALS, THE TENDER VERTIGO THAT ASPHYXIATES, A WHIPWORM IN THE THROAT, THE KISS OF PHOSPHORESCENT SHACKLES IN ICY AMNIOTIC SUSPENSION.

DRAGGED INTO A POROUS, MEPHITIC ANTE-CHAMBER; STENCH OF COCKROACHES, QUICKLIME AND DUNG. THE CARCASS-KEEPER OF THE FEMALE BUTCHERS, GNASHING ON CUDS OF GENITAL GRISTLE; CLUTCHING CRYPT-KEYS TO HIS BELT; COWERING BEHIND HIS SIBILANT, TWO-TONGUED MISTRESS - PANDORA, QUEEN OF THE CRIMSON NIGHT!
TWO HEADS IN BLACK WATER. NO BODIES. NIGHT FIGURES CUT FROM A STONE CASCADE. REAL VAMPIRES PACK HEAT FROM A SUGAR HOLE, DRINK MENSTRUAL BLOOD, EVERY BITCH A MEAT BOTTLE SWIGGED AT THE NECK OF THE WOMB. FUCKING IS FOR DOGS.
LITTLE GIRL, LITTLE GIRL, MY MINIONS ARE GRAVEWORMS IN HUMAN GUISE. LITTLE GIRL, WATCH YOUR DREAMS DEVOURED AND SKULL-CREAMED TO SHRIEKING ASH. THEY SUCK THE SLIME FROM YOUR BODY, SPEW IT ON A SCARECROW OF THORNS.
I SEE THUNDERHEADS OVER PLAINS OF HALF-EATEN LIGHT AND KNIFED INCUBUS BONE. FLASHBACK TO CUT-THROAT CASTLE, GIRLS SHIT FOR SATAN SHIT FOR ANYONE, SIX-INCH SILVER SLIDE TO MIDNIGHT, PENTAGRAMS OF DEMON DUST ON CLIT ON CLAW.
THE SOFT EMBRACE OF A DEATH MACHINE. BLACK FUR, BLACK EYES, BLACK SPERM.
I DREAMT I ATE A WOLF.

CORPSEFUCKER BLUES

MUD IN TORRENTS, WORMS IN THE MUD, IN EVERY WORM THE PRIMAL HELIX OF FUTURE LIFE. A MILLION YEARS OF RAIN. THEN THE SUN ASCENDS, EVAPORATING OCEANS. FISH CAST ASHORE TO WRITHE ON BELLIES, GROW LIMBS, SHED SCALES, GROW FUR WHILE THE EARTH'S CRUST GRINDS, CRACKS AND EJACULATES COLUMNS OF MAGMA. CITIES CUT FROM ROCK, FROM BLOOD, FROM HUMAN SACRIFICE. EVERY BONEYARD A GATE OF FIRE THROUGH WHICH EACH MUST PASS WHO SEEKS HIS TRUE AND ANCIENT PARENTAGE.
MY MOTHER NAMED ME GUILLAUME, BUT MY FORMER MASTER, THE DUC DE BLANGIS, CALLED ME ASS-DESTROYER. THE WINTER OF 1795 WE SPENT IN HIS CHATEAU OF SELLIGNY, HIGH IN THE SNOW-COVERED MOUNTAINS; IT WAS A SEASON OF TORTURE, MURDER, ANNIHILATION. MY JOB WAS THAT OF CHIEF ANUS-RAPER FOR THE DUC; ON HIS COMMAND I WOULD PENETRATE, LACERATE, EVISCERATE, DEVASTATE.
IN MARCH, AS THE FIRST SNOWS MELTED, WE FEW SURVIVORS LEFT THE CHATEAU. THE DESCENT TOOK SEVERAL DAYS; ON THE THIRD, AS WE PASSED THROUGH SWATHES OF DENSE FOREST, OUR BAND WAS ATTACKED BY RAVENING WOLVES.
I SAVED THE DUC'S LIFE, BUT SUSTAINED TERRIBLE BITES TO MY HANDS, MY FACE, MY COCK. FOR WEEKS I LAY IN PARIS WITH A DEATHLY AGUE.
WHEN I AWOKE, MY APPETITES WERE ALL BUT UNGOVERNABLE.

MUCH TO MY MASTER'S AMUSEMENT, I NOW NOT ONLY HAD AN UNCONTROLLABLE URGE TO BUGGER THE MUTILATED VICTIMS HE PROVIDED, BUT ALSO TO FALL UPON THEIR BLOODY HAUNCHES AFTERWARDS AND CONSUME THEM LIKE A RABID DOG. MY VISAGE, MY TALONS, MY VERY LIFE WAS A RED RUINS OF SPERM-RIMED SPHINCTERS, SHREDDED GUTS, AND PULSATING FAECAL MEAT.

FINALLY, REVOLUTIONARIES ARRESTED BLANGIS, DRAGGED HIM TO THE GUILLOTINE, AND CHOPPED OFF HIS HEAD. I WAS FREE... BUT FREE TO GO WHERE, TO DO WHAT?

MY DESIRES LED ME TO THE ONLY SANCTUARY PARIS COULD PROVIDE – THE MIDNIGHT GRAVEYARD. HERE I DWELT IN SHADOWS, PREYING ON THE WARMEST OF CORPSES MY CLAWS COULD UNEARTH, SODOMISING, RIPPING AND DEVOURING.

IN THAT WAY I SURVIVED FOR DECADES – BUT THERE WERE OTHERS LIKE ME, THEY GREW CARELESS: BERTRAND, WHO FELL UNCONSCIOUS OVER A PILE OF RAVAGED LIMBS, AND ARDISSON, WHO TOOK HOME THE HEAD OF A RIPE ROTTING GIRL AND PLAYED WITH IT UNTIL IT DISINTEGRATED. THE AUTHORITIES CLAMPED DOWN IN SWARMS, CRUCIFYING THE NIGHT, DRIVING ME INTO THE MADDENING SUN.

AND SO I TOOK A PLAGUE-SHIP AND FLED TO NEW ORLEANS.

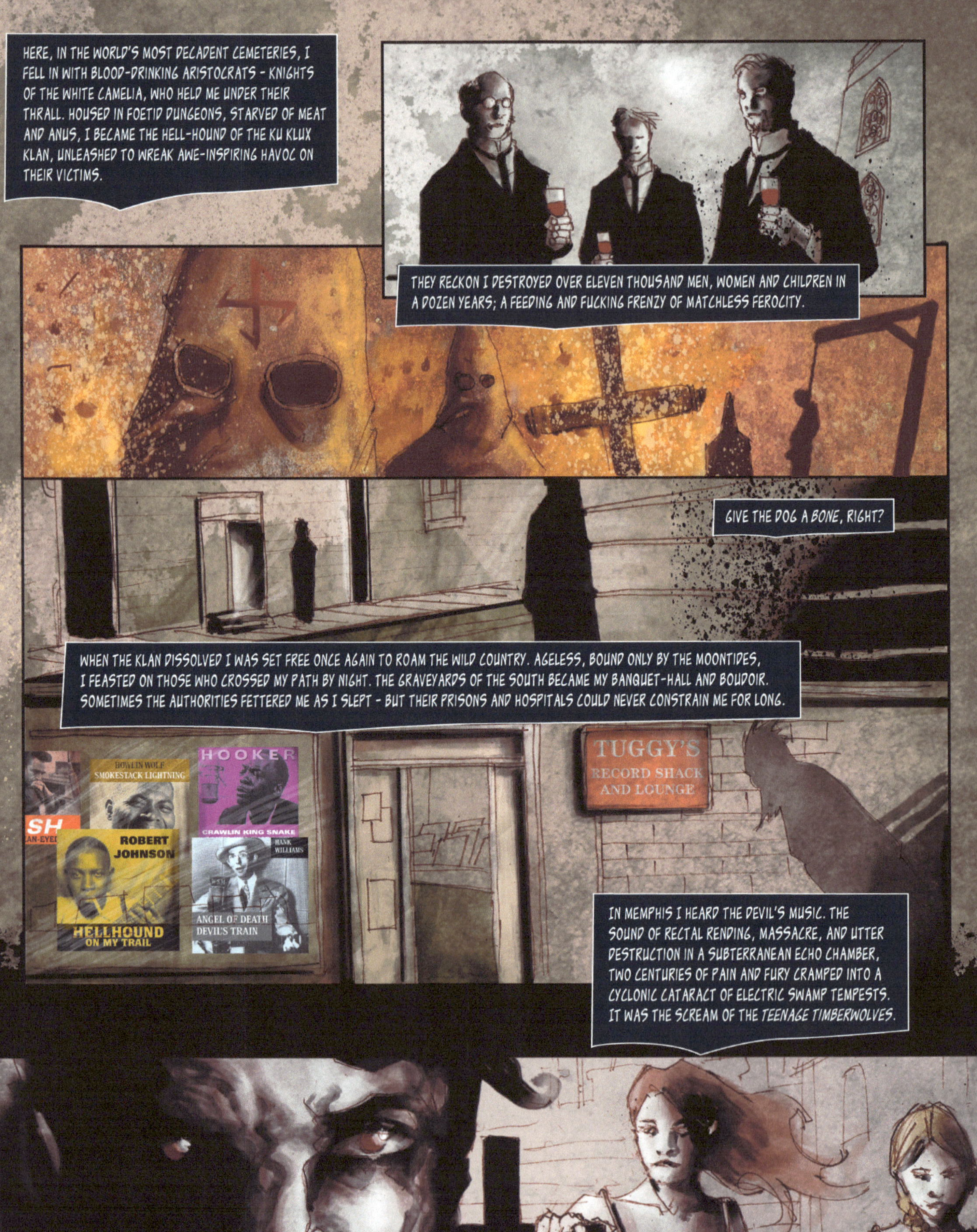

HERE, IN THE WORLD'S MOST DECADENT CEMETERIES, I FELL IN WITH BLOOD-DRINKING ARISTOCRATS – KNIGHTS OF THE WHITE CAMELIA, WHO HELD ME UNDER THEIR THRALL. HOUSED IN FOETID DUNGEONS, STARVED OF MEAT AND ANUS, I BECAME THE HELL-HOUND OF THE KU KLUX KLAN, UNLEASHED TO WREAK AWE-INSPIRING HAVOC ON THEIR VICTIMS.
THEY RECKON I DESTROYED OVER ELEVEN THOUSAND MEN, WOMEN AND CHILDREN IN A DOZEN YEARS; A FEEDING AND FUCKING FRENZY OF MATCHLESS FEROCITY.
GIVE THE DOG A BONE, RIGHT?
WHEN THE KLAN DISSOLVED I WAS SET FREE ONCE AGAIN TO ROAM THE WILD COUNTRY. AGELESS, BOUND ONLY BY THE MOONTIDES, I FEASTED ON THOSE WHO CROSSED MY PATH BY NIGHT. THE GRAVEYARDS OF THE SOUTH BECAME MY BANQUET-HALL AND BOUDOIR. SOMETIMES THE AUTHORITIES FETTERED ME AS I SLEPT – BUT THEIR PRISONS AND HOSPITALS COULD NEVER CONSTRAIN ME FOR LONG.
HOWLIN WOLF
SMOKESTACK LIGHTNING
HOOKER
SH
AN-EYED
ROBERT JOHNSON
CRAWLIN KING SNAKE
HANK WILLIAMS
HELLHOUND ON MY TRAIL
ANGEL OF DEATH
DEVIL'S TRAIN
TUGGY'S
RECORD SHACK AND LOUNGE
IN MEMPHIS I HEARD THE DEVIL'S MUSIC. THE SOUND OF RECTAL RENDING, MASSACRE, AND UTTER DESTRUCTION IN A SUBTERRANEAN ECHO CHAMBER, TWO CENTURIES OF PAIN AND FURY CRAMPED INTO A CYCLONIC CATARACT OF ELECTRIC SWAMP TEMPESTS. IT WAS THE SCREAM OF THE TEENAGE TIMBERWOLVES.
SATURN HANGS IN RETROGRADE, THE HORNED ONE COUNTS HIS STINKING GOLD.
TERROR TAKES THE THRONE WHEN THE THREE SIXES CLASH.
IT'S TIME TO EAT SOME ASS!

CHAPTER FOUR

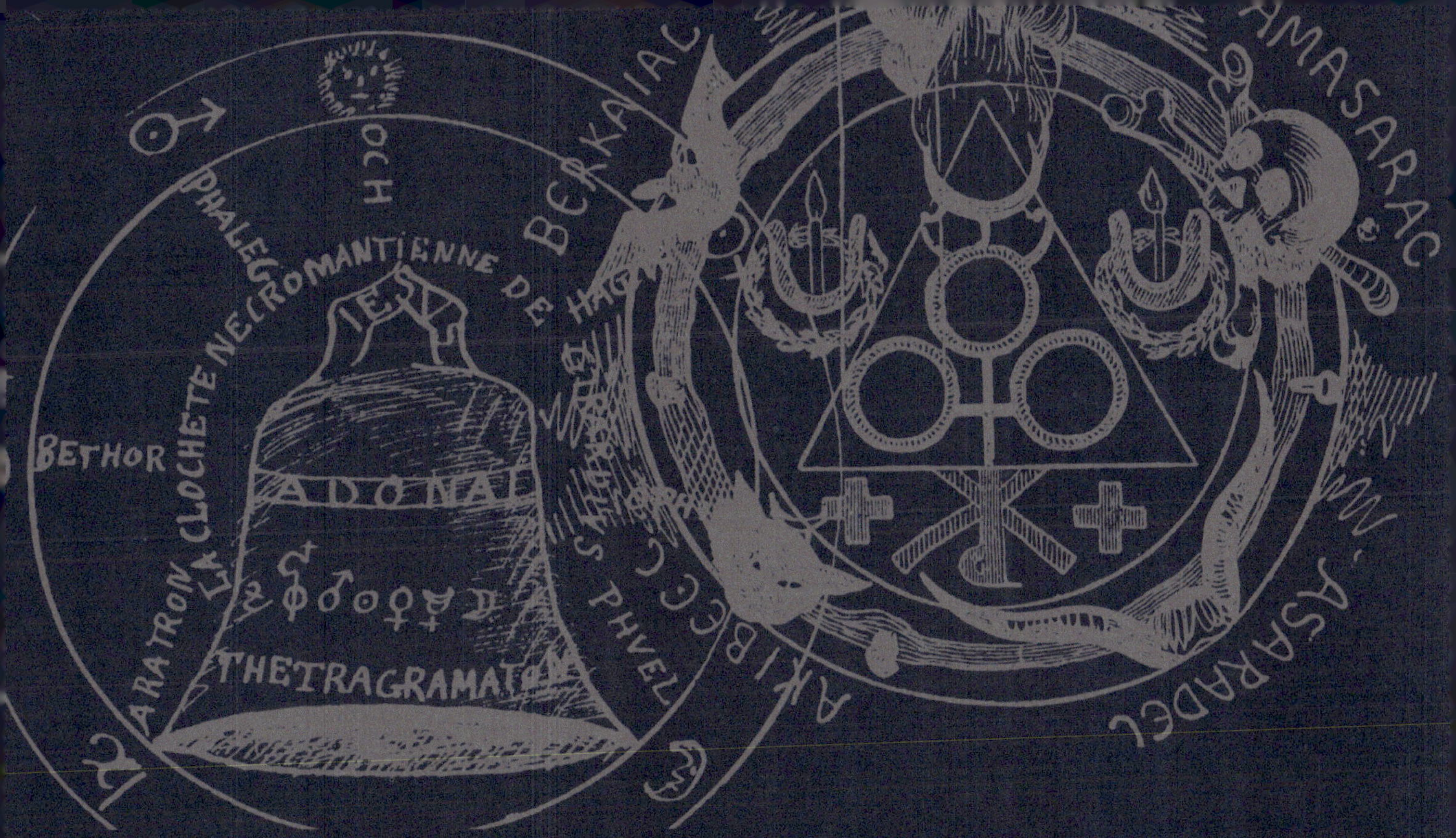

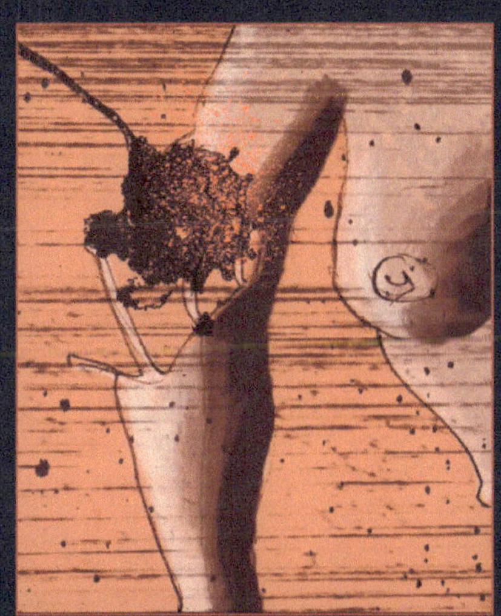

ASSASSINS OF GHOST-CAT CASTLE

WHILE CANDY WAITS BENEATH BOREAL AUSPICES, WE TRACK THE SCENT OF YUKI'S WOMB-BLOOD IN THE BREEZE. A MILLION MENSTRUATING GIRLS IN THE FAR-OFF CITY, AND EACH ONE SUBTLY DIFFERENT.
ABOVE, THE FIRMAMENT AN EBON MIRROR LACED WITH PROWLING SPIKES OF LIGHT, ASTRAL CINCTURES BINDING US TO A COVENANT WITH CRIME. THE DESERTSCAPE IS PHANTASMIC, A CENTURIED HALLUCINATION IN THE TETHERED MINDS OF DOGS WHO HUNTED PRIMEVAL TUNDRAS WHERE THE EARTH THREW FORMS OF BOILING ROCK IN CONTEST WITH THE LAVAL SKY, LASHED BY LEATHER WINGS, INSECT FORCEPS, PITHS OF SNAKING SULPHUR. A DIM RED RICTUS OF DUNES AND SKULLTOOTH FOSSIL RAMPARTS RISES, MOTHER MASTIFFS YOWL AS IF NIGHTMARE HOOVES ARE PLANING THE SOFT ANVIL OF THEIR GUTS, DOUBLE-UDDERED FLANKS AND HINDS CREVICED TO THE VERY BONE WITH VULVAS BLEEDING BILE.
SUNKEN PSALMS NICHED IN ROCKFACE, A MENAGERIE OF MIGRANT SHADES AUTHORING OBLIVION ON MORTAL THOUGHT, ANNEALING OUR ABJECT DESOLATION.
WHITE SCORPIONS LIGHT THE WAY, HEX-SHAPED HEARTS AGLOW BENEATH THEIR WAFER-PLATED SACS, REFRACTING THE MACH OF ALGOL'S CRYPTIC SPECTRA. A NUCLEAR NEXUS, A COAGULATION-POINT FOR THE MEMORY OF GALAXIES, A CHASM OF RAVENOUS SPACE THROUGH WHICH WE THREAD LIKE CANKERS IN THE MARROW OF MYTHIC MAYHEM. OUR SOULS AS GAUNT AS SAURIAN SCAPULAS BLEACHED AEONS-LONG ON SHALES OF WAN PRE-HUMAN CLINKER, OUR ACCURSED TRANSIT SHADOWPLAY, A PHOSPHOROUS AFTERBURN GLIMPSED IN THE SOCKETS OF ARACHNID HEADBONES; WE HUNGER.

THE TRAIL ENDS HERE. A CHARNEL HOUSE, ITS AURA PREGNANT WITH LIQUEFACTION, RANK WITH GLUTTED CARRION FLIES AND THEIR ADDLED EGGS; A CASTELLATED CATAFALQUE FOR UNDEAD BRIDES.

BELLADONNA WREATHES ITS PORTALS, DOORS OF MOON-KISSED OAK THAT CAVE INWARDS UNDER BILLY'S BOOT-HEEL WITH THE SICKLY SUSURRATION OF DISEASED LABIA.

A STENCH OF DANK SOIL, LEAVENED WITH SUGARED COPPER AND AMMONIA. UNDER THE FILMY GAZE OF LONG-EXTINGUISHED EYES. AND A BALEFUL, CLIMACTIC CHITTERING.

RATS.

NO MISTAKE. THESE MUST BE THE PESTILENTIAL FAMILIARS OF PANDORA'S PERSONAL GUARD OF ZIPPER VIXENS ELITE...

...THE SEVEN BRIDES OF BELPHEGOR!
WANDA, WICKED WITCH OF CUT-THROAT CASTLE.
HI, I'M HONEY. I LIKE HEAD.
I'M JEZEBEL - I BITE.

I'M CARMILLA, KEEPER OF THE SCARAB SCUM.
HI, I'M AURORA, AND I'LL DRINK ANYTHING.
LOVECHILD - I WAS MADE IN THE SHADE.
MADONNA, MISTRESS OF THE MAGGOT MINX.

SEVEN BRIDES, SEVEN BULLETS...
...SEVEN BLOODY BUTTHOLES FOR BILLY!
BILLY'S EYES IGNITE WITH THE GELATINOUS FLARE OF ONE WHO HAS NAVIGATED CENTURIES OF NIGHT TO RECEIVE A LEPER'S KISS IN A THORN GARDEN; TEETH, CLAWS, AND COCK PLOUGH INTO GAPING WOUND TRACTS AS AUTOMATIC GUNFIRE STRAFES THE CEILING AND WALLS. THE STING OF HOT LEAD ONLY DRIVES HIM TO MORE FRENZIED TRUCIDATIONS, THE RELIGIOUS ECSTASY OF GENOCIDE.
THESE BLOODSUCKER BITCHES ARE PUTRID TO THE CORE; GUTS LATTICED BY CENTIPEDES AND THICK BLACK LEECHES, MARBLED FLESH REAMING APART SPURTING RANCID PUS OF GANGRENE AND GONHORREA, COLD STAGNANT BLOOD, COLD SHIT IN HORN-SHAPED FOSSILISED STOOLS. BLADDER-STONES CLATTER ACROSS THE ART-DECO FLOOR. WHAT A STINKING FUCKING MESS.

THE BRIDAL SUITE STRIPPED BARE. YUKI WAS HERE... BUT NOW?

AT FIRST THE HUNCHBACK DOESN'T TALK. UNTIL I DIG OUT HIS LEFT TESTICLE AND BILLY SETS FIRE TO THE SPERM DUCTS.

THE CHARRED BONE-BLANCHER ROILS WITH A GLUTINOUS VULTURE CROAKING. "RATTLESNAKE INN, ROUTE 23." IN THE SHADOW OF THE GALLOWS POLE, HEADING SOUTH-EAST TO BAYOU COUNTRY, THE CALL OF THE CRIMSON NIGHT.

GIVE ME BLOODCLOTS, LIVERS AND LARD, THE SUCKLEBONES OF A DWARF.

SCORPIO BURNS IN THE BELLY OF THE BEAST THAT BIT ME.

SOMEONE COULD GET SKINNED.

THE WEDDING CHAPEL'S EPICENTRAL CHAMBER IS LINED WITH COFFIN-WOOD AND HUMAN MEAT OVER SHEET IRON; AN ORGONE ACCUMULATOR WITH THE CAPACITY TO REGENERATE MORBID TISSUE IN ITS VAGINO-PLASMIC ENERGY FIELD. BENEATH HERE LIES PANDORA'S VAULTED CRYPT, STORED WITH THE REMAINS OF HUNDREDS OF MEN METICULOUSLY PARED DOWN INTO SMOKE-CURED SKINS, DESICCATED MUSCULATURE, BONES PICKED CLEAN, ORGANS IN VATS, ROW AFTER ROW OF SEVERED GENITALS IN JARS.

HORROR HOSPITAL.

A GIRL COULD FEEL AT HOME HERE.

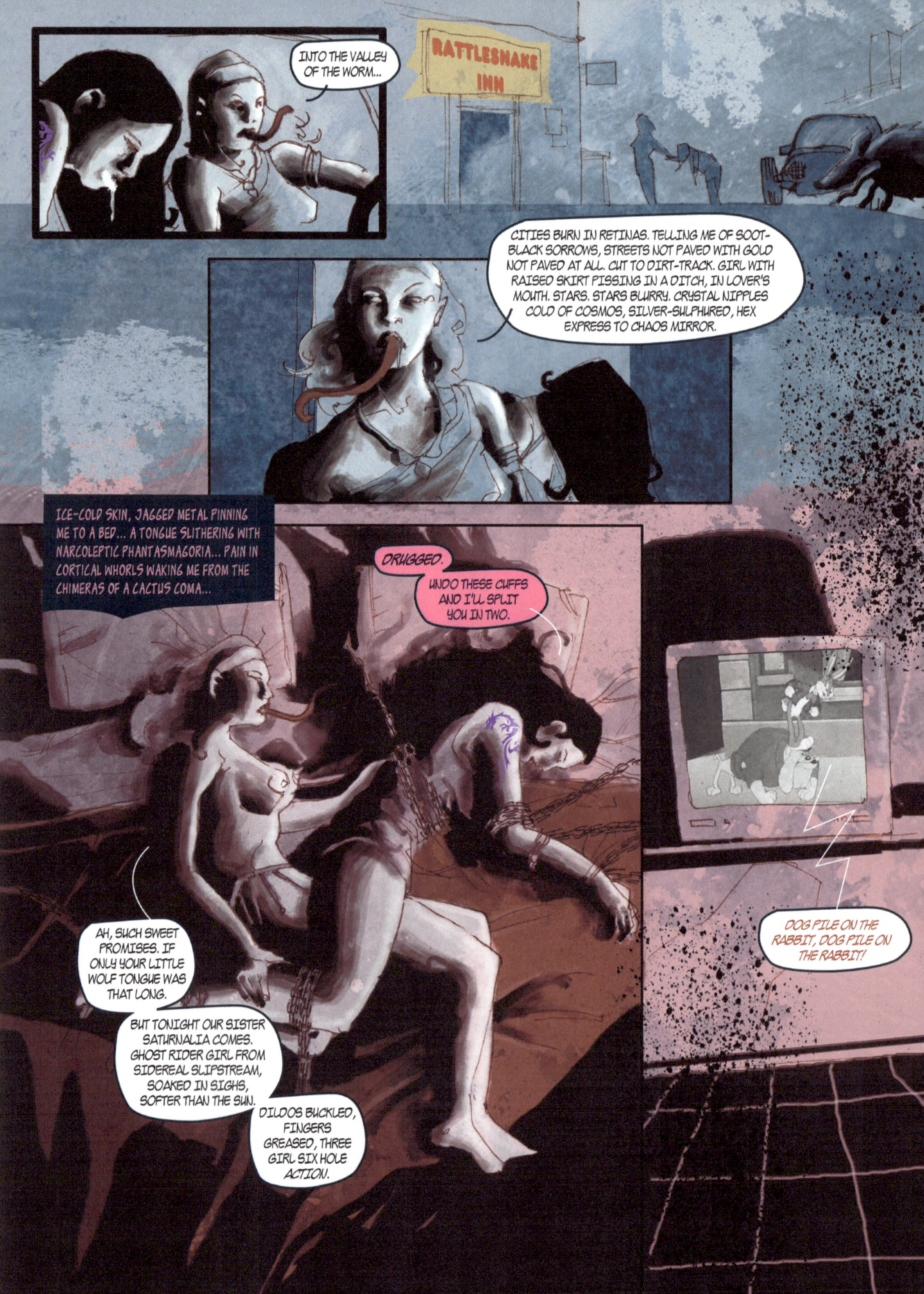

INTO THE VALLEY OF THE WORM...
RATTLESNAKE INN
CITIES BURN IN RETINAS. TELLING ME OF SOOT-BLACK SORROWS, STREETS NOT PAVED WITH GOLD NOT PAVED AT ALL. CUT TO DIRT-TRACK. GIRL WITH RAISED SKIRT PISSING IN A DITCH, IN LOVER'S MOUTH. STARS. STARS BLURRY. CRYSTAL NIPPLES COLD OF COSMOS, SILVER-SULPHURED, HEX EXPRESS TO CHAOS MIRROR.
ICE-COLD SKIN, JAGGED METAL PINNING ME TO A BED... A TONGUE SLITHERING WITH NARCOLEPTIC PHANTASMAGORIA... PAIN IN CORTICAL WHORLS WAKING ME FROM THE CHIMERAS OF A CACTUS COMA...
DRUGGED.
UNDO THESE CUFFS AND I'LL SPLIT YOU IN TWO.
AH, SUCH SWEET PROMISES. IF ONLY YOUR LITTLE WOLF TONGUE WAS THAT LONG.
BUT TONIGHT OUR SISTER SATURNALIA COMES. GHOST RIDER GIRL FROM SIDEREAL SLIPSTREAM, SOAKED IN SIGHS, SOFTER THAN THE SUN.
DILDOS BUCKLED, FINGERS GREASED, THREE GIRL SIX HOLE ACTION.
DOG PILE ON THE RABBIT, DOG PILE ON THE RABBIT!

SATURNALIA. QUEEN OF THE VELVET VOID, ELDEST OF THE SEVEN SISTERS WHO HOLD DOMINION OVER *NOSFERATU NATION*.

ELEMENTAL, VICIOUS, VAINGLORIOUS; BEHIND HER EYES, AN INSATIABLE GOAD TO GRATIFICATION.

BENEATH HER FINGERNAILS, THE RUINS OF A STARGAZER.

FOUR HEADSTONE HANDS PROBING, PERFORATING MY BODY AS IT SWIRLS NUMBLY AT THE FREEZING-POINT OF PELTS, MY MIND SHORT-CIRCUITED BY PSYCHOTROPIC TRIGGERS, PROMPTING A PROCESSION OF FLASH-FRAMED, FORMATIVE MEMORIES FROM MY TRANSIENT EXISTENCE...

AFTER THE DEATH OF MY PARENTS, I WAS ASSIGNED TO THE CUSTODY OF MY GRANDFATHER, WHO LIVED ON THE SHORES OF SADOGASHIMA IN A FORTRESS OF CONVOLUTED JADE KNOWN AS "GHOST-CAT CASTLE".

ALTHOUGH THE SAMURAI CASTE WAS OUTLAWED IN 1876, MANY OF ITS MEMBERS FORMED SMALL, CLANDESTINE ORDERS WHICH PERSISTED IN THE SHADOWS. I WAS SOON TO LEARN THAT SADOGASHIMA WAS HOME TO THE MOST SECRET AND DEADLY OF THESE COVERT SOCIETIES, THE *SHINZANSATSU* CLAN, AND THAT MY GRANDFATHER – FORMERLY CHIEF EXECUTIONER TO THE SHOGUN, AND KNOWN AS "LORD SHURA" – WAS ITS LEADER.

DESPITE BEING OVER NINETY YEARS OLD, MY GRANDFATHER BOASTED EXTRAORDINARY PHYSICAL POWERS. AS A LOVER, HE MAINTAINED A PERMANENT ERECTION AND COULD EJACULATE SEVEN TIMES IN SEVEN MINUTES WITHOUT DIMINUTION; AS A KILLER, HE HAD PERFECTED TECHNIQUES TO DECAPITATE THREE OPPONENTS WITH A SINGLE SWORDSTROKE, AND TO STRIP THE LIVING FLESH FROM A MAN'S SKULL WITH HIS BARE HANDS IN LESS THAN A SECOND.

AT THE FIRST ONSET OF PUBERTY, I BEGAN MY INITIATION INTO THE WAYS OF SEX AND THE SAMURAI. I WAS ELEVEN YEARS OLD.

WHEN I WAS THIRTEEN, A LOCAL SNAKE-BUTCHER ATTACKED AND TRIED TO RAPE ME, BELIEVING MY GRANDFATHER TOO OLD AND FEEBLE TO INTERVENE. LORD SHURA TORE OFF THE WRETCH'S FACE WITH ONE INTRICATE, DOUBLE-HANDED STRIKE, A SOLITARY EYEBALL LEFT TWITCHING ON A PULP OF CALAMITOUS GRISTLE.

THAT MOMENT SAW THE BIRTH OF MY THIRST FOR THE BEAUTIFUL, VERMILION FLOWERS OF *CARNAGE*.

BY SEVENTEEN I HAD MASTERED THE SWORD. IT WAS JUST BEFORE MY BIRTHDAY THAT THE *SHINZANSATSU* CLAN ABDUCTED, TORTURED AND DISEMBOWELLED A DOZEN CORRUPT GOVERNMENT OFFICIALS; MY GRANDFATHER AWARDED ME THE HONOUR OF HARVESTING THEIR HEADS.

NOW ONE HUNDRED AND TWO YEARS OLD, LORD SHURA WAS READY TO FULFIL HIS LONG-BURNING AMBITION TO USURP THE JAPANESE GOVERNMENT AND RESTORE HIS HOMELAND TO THE RULE OF *BUSHIDO* AND *HAGAKURE*, THE GLORIOUS CODES OF THE SAMURAI. FEARING FOR MY SAFETY IN THE EVENT OF CIVIL WAR, HE ORDERED ME TO AMERICA WHERE I WAS TO AWAIT MY SUMMONS TO RETURN.

FROM THE AIRPORT LOUNGE I WATCHED ON TELEVISION AS *SHINZANSATSU* WARRIORS STORMED THE *DIET* BUILDING AND LORD SHURA TOOK THE BALCONY TO ADDRESS THE GATHERING CROWDS BELOW, HIS REVOLUTIONARY DIATRIBE PUNCTUATED BY THE HURLING OF ROTTING PARLIAMENTARIAN HEADS. BUT LORD SHURA WAS A PROPHET OUT OF TIME; HIS WORDS AND ACTIONS WERE GREETED FIRST WITH REVULSION, THEN WITH RIDICULE.

I WAS THIRTY SECONDS OVER TOKYO WHEN THE *SHINZANSATSU* CLAN EXTERMINATED THEMSELVES IN A MASS, CHOREOGRAPHED AND LIVE-TELEVISED ACT OF BLOODY RITUAL *SEPPUKU*.

ALONE IN CALIFORNIA, I WANDERED THE DESERT IN MOURNING. HERE I ENCOUNTERED AN OCCULT SECT OF HIPPIES, DRUG-DEALERS, RAMRODDERS AND CUM-WITCHES WHO FUCKED AND DRANK COYOTE BLOOD IN PSYCHEDELIC MOON ORGIES.

ON THE NINETY-THIRD DAY, SADIE WILL BECOME PUSSYCAT'S WIFE, AND PUSSYCAT WILL BE SODOMISED BY SHORTY. SADIE WILL BEAR THE MARK OF SHE WHO RUNS NAKED WITH THE DOGS.
THIS IS THE WILL OF THE LOCUSTS OF THE PIT.
SO MOTE IT BE.

SAN JOSE

I LIVED WITH THEM FOR A YEAR; THEY TAUGHT ME HOW TO SPEAK ENGLISH, AND IN RETURN I SHOWED THEM THE ART OF BUTCHERING HUMANS.

AFTER THAT, I WAS A PAID ASSASSIN FOR THE HELL'S ANGELS; MY LAST HIT WAS AT ALTAMONT SPEEDWAY.

BUT MY LUST FOR BLOOD WAS MATCHED ONLY BY A LONGING FOR MY OWN NULLIFICATION; AND SO I DRIFTED ON THROUGH THE DARKLANDS, SEARCHING FOR THE SKELETON RECOIL OF ABANDON.

BROTHERS AND SISTERS OF THE NEW REVELATIONS, WE ARE GATHERED HERE TODAY TO PRAY FOR THE SOUL OF OUR LOST DAUGHTER, CANDICE.
VENEREAL NIGHT-BUTCHERS SNATCHED HER FROM BESIDE HER MOTHER'S RESTING-PLACE AS A STORM SPAT RAPING FLAMES AND WATERSPOUTS WHIRLED AT THE FIRST CONSCIOUSNESS OF CHAOS.
NOW SHE DWELLS IN THE VALE OF SATYRS, A BOLT-BLASTED CUR-SLUT OF THE PRIAPIC PERMANOX.
IT IS WRITTEN IN BLOOD PSALM 23, THE SCRIPTURE OF THE BEAST THAT RISES FROM ITS OWN ANUS: "A CARNAL, BOOMING WIND, HEAVY WITH BRIMSTONE. THE AIR MEASURABLE AND GRINDING, BUT WITH NO PENETRABLE FORM. ITS EYE A MOSAIC OF BURSTS, A SORT OF HARD COSMIC HAMMER DISTORTED BY WEIGHT, CEASELESSLY DROPPING LIKE A BROW IN SPACE, WITH A SEEMINGLY DISTILLED SOUND, A HUGE INFLUX OF VEGETAL THUNDERING BLOOD..."
SATAN'S COCK, THE RED RAMROD...
IT BURNS, IT BLISTERS...
THE ROTTEN EYE THAT SHOOTS BLACK BLOOD INSIDE...
SATAN'S BABY, MADE OF SHIT...
FLAYED BY THE LORD OF WHIPS...

CHURCH
RING
SHOULD WE INCREASE THE PREACHER'S DOSAGE?
PERHAPS SHE AND HER FRIENDS WOULD LIKE TO COME AND STAY.
KAMP
KINO
CHURCH
RING
NO. I LIKE THE WAY HE'S TALKING.
IN FACT, I'M THINKING OF PUTTING HIM ON REAL LIVE TELEVISION. A MISSION OF MERCY, AN APPEAL TO HIS MISSING CHILD.
THE TRAUMA OF LOSING HIS WIFE DURING CHILDBIRTH, FOLLOWED BY THE KIDNAPPING OF HIS DAUGHTER BY A GANG OF GRAVEROBBERS, SENT PREACHER CARRION OVER THE EDGE. HE HAD ALREADY FORMULATED HIS SO-CALLED NEW REVELATIONS OF BEING, IN WHICH AN ORGANLESS HUMAN ANATOMY FUSES WITH THE ROOT MATTER OF PROTOSTARS.
IN HIS MIND, EXCREMENT NOW BECAME THE HOLY HOST, THE MISSING LINK BETWEEN BASE HUMANITY AND HIS FUTURE FORM AS A PRISTINE COSMIC PROPHET.
A REGULAR DOGHOLE MESSIAH.
WHITE CAMELIA MENTAL INSTITUTE
"...IN THE THROBBING OF THE SOLITARY NIGHT, THAT ANT-LIKE NOISE OCCURS WHICH DISCOVERIES, REVELATIONS, AND APPARITIONS MAKE, THESE GREAT ABORTIVE BODIES TAKING WIND AND WING AGAIN, THE IMMENSE QUIVERING OF THIS CONVENTION OF CORPSES."

SUN COMES UP, ANOTHER DAY BEGINS. AND I'M ALL ALONE, HITCHING A RIDE INTO LIGHTNING COUNTRY. HE SMELLS LIKE BARBECUE AND BAD GUMS, KIND OF SQUIRLY AND UNFOCUSED IN THE DEAD CENTRE OF THINGS. CARIL WOULD JUST TAKE THAT RIFLE AND BLOW HIS BRAINS OUT, STEAL HIS TRUCK; BUT I'M ONLY A LITTLE GIRL... WHICH IS PROBABLY WHY THE CREEP LIKES ME.
"SWEET HOME ALABAMA..."
TOOK THE EARS CLEAN OFF A JACKRABBIT.
TIME FER SOME COFFEE 'N' GRITS.
MAX'S
ROADKILL CITY
IT'S ALL GOOD, BABY.
HOW'S ABOUT YOU AN' ME STEPPIN' OUT SOMETIME...
...I GOT THE WHEELS IF YOU GOT THE SQUEALS.
WHEN HELL FREEZES OVER.
MORE COFFEE, MISS?
OH MY GOD... THE TV...

...DADDY??
...WHEN YOU COME HOME, CANDY. MAMA'S WAITING IN THE FIERY PLACE, WITH VENOM IN HER VEINS JUST FOR YOU.
JUST REMEMBER WHAT IT SAYS IN THE BIBLE, SWEETHEART: "MY MENTAL ARTERIES WILL BE MELTED IN QUICKLIME, THEN MY BESTIARY WILL BE ASCENDENT AND MY MYSTIQUE WILL HAVE BECOME A SHIELD. THEN THE JOINTS IN THE STONES WILL APPEAR, FUMING, AND ARBOREAL BUNCHES OF MIND'S EYE WILL SET INTO GLOSSARIES AND STONE AEROLITHS WILL FALL..."
"...THEN LINES WILL APPEAR, THEN NON-SPATIAL GEOMETRIES WILL BE UNDERSTOOD AND PEOPLE WILL LEARN WHAT THE CONFIGURATION OF MIND MEANS AND THEY WILL UNDERSTAND HOW I LOST MY MIND."
I FEEL A DOG DAWN RISING, SPRUNG JAWS THAT SLAVER, ACCELERATING PHALLIC HEAT.
LITTLE GIRL, BULLETS AND BLADES CAN NEVER STAUNCH THE POWER OF PUSSY-QUEEN. YOUR DEMON BROTHER COMES FOR YOU, BUT IN HIS DARK HEART HE DREAMS OF PANDORA. THE MARROW-BONES ARE IN THE TROUGH...
PUPPY WANTS TO FUCK.
GENTLEMEN, LET ME TELL YOU A SCARY STORY...
... ABOUT THINGS THAT SALIVATE AND SIDLE IN THE MOST ABJECT CREVICES OF CREATION...
KINO
I THOUGHT MY DADDY WAS DEAD, THAT THEY COOKED HIM IN THE CHAIR... THE DAY THE PRISON AMBULANCE CAME AND TOOK HIM AWAY, THEY SAID HE WAS GUILTY OF BLACK MAGIC, THAT HE POISONED OLD MRS SCROLLIVER DEAD WITH A EUCHARIST OF DUNG, TURNED HER INSIDES INTO THE DEVIL'S DITCHWATER.
TWO WEEKS LATER I MET MY NEW FAMILY, THE ONES WHO PREY AND PLAY WITH THUNDERBOLTS. SO WHERE DO I GO NOW?
WHAT DOES IT MEAN FOR A LIVING PERSON TO CONFRONT DEATH? ACCORDING TO HAGAKURE, THE CODEX OF THE SAMURAI, WHAT IS IMPORTANT IS PURITY OF ACTION. EVEN AS LIFE MEANS NOTHING, AND ALL THINGS END IN NOTHING, SO THE WAY OF THE SAMURAI IS ALWAYS DEATH. THAT'S WHAT MY GRANDFATHER TAUGHT ME – AND THAT'S WHAT I'M GOING TO TEACH THAT CERVIX-SUCKING DYKE PANDORA.

CHAPTER FIVE

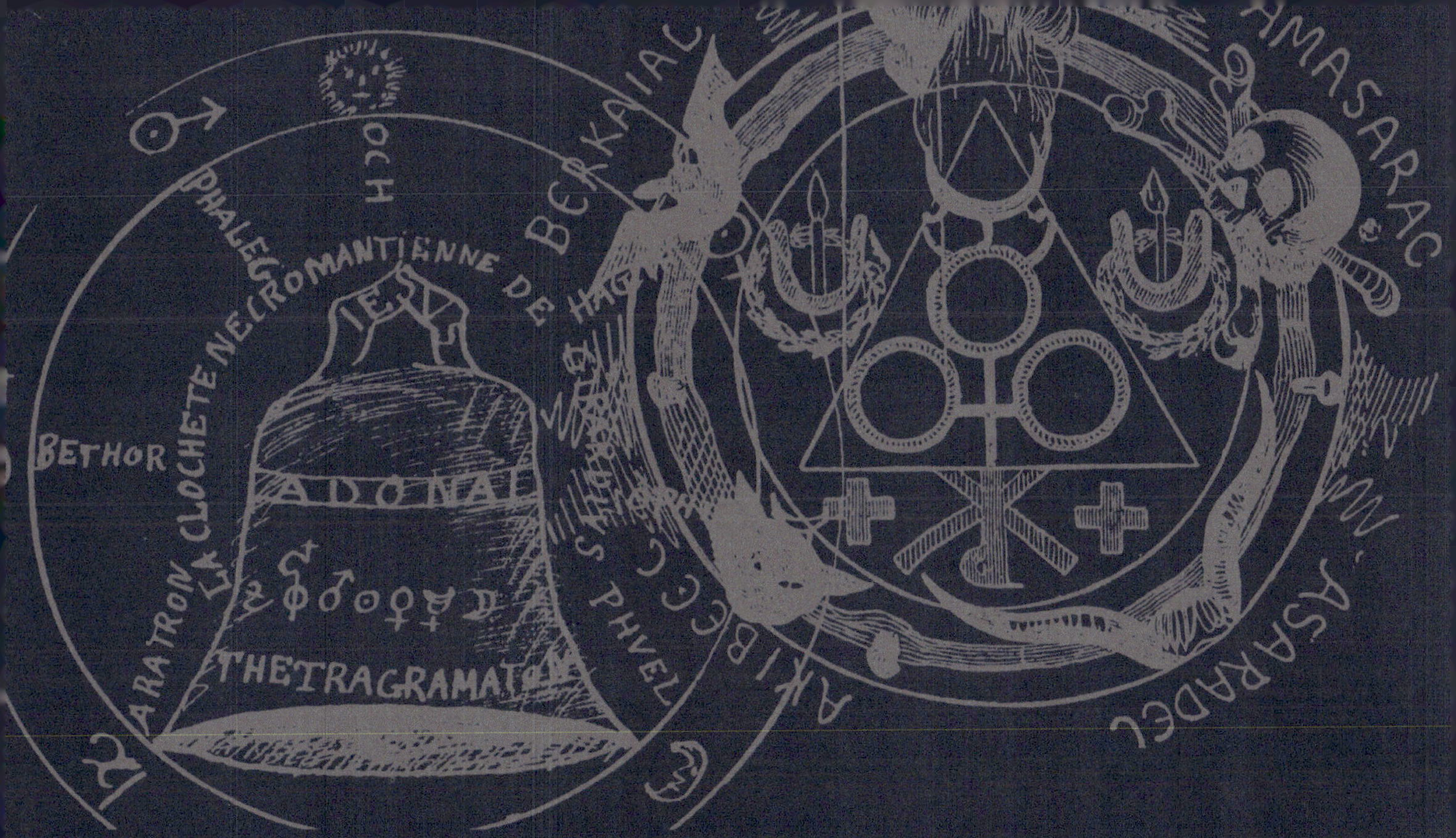

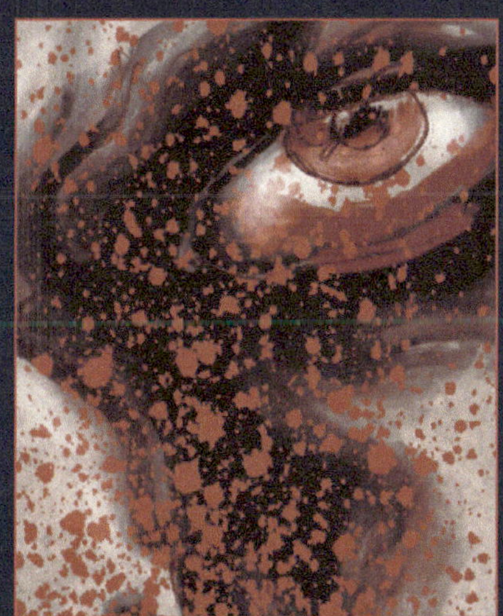

FUNERAL ASYLUM OF WHIPS

"FREAKS ON ACID. THE LAST OF THE UNDERGROUND MONSTER SHOWS, TOURING THE BIBLE BELT BY COVER OF NIGHT, SETTING UP IN CLANDESTINE CATTLE-SHACKS WHERE RELIGIOUS REDNECKS COULD MOCK AND VILIFY THE ABOMINATIONS OF THE LORD."
"REVEREND ASHTON, THE RINGMASTER AND WRANGLER, WOULD DOSE HIS DEFORMED SLAVES WITH LSD AND THEN LET THEM LOOSE IN THE TINY ARENA. SURROUNDED BY BAYING DRUNKS, GNARLING UNDER ASHTON'S LASH, THE HAPLESS CREATURES WOULD CAVORT IN A GURGLING, WRITHING, FESTERING BACCHANALE OF THE CRIPPLED AND CONVULSIVE INSANE."
"FINALLY, THE ACID OVERDOSES LED TO MASS PSYCHOSIS; ONE STORM-STREAKED NIGHT THE FREAKS, LED BY ONE PAPA LOBSTER, TURNED ON THEIR KEEPER, BELIEVING HIM TO BE SAINT SEBASTIANE OF SEWERS, AND CRUCIFIED HIM ON A BOXCAR ALONG WITH A PAIR OF LOCAL PROSTITUTES, WHO THEY DEEMED HIS DARKSIDE SERAPHS OF EXCREMENTITION."
"THE PAPERS CALLED IT THE JESUS TRAIN WHORE MASSACRE."

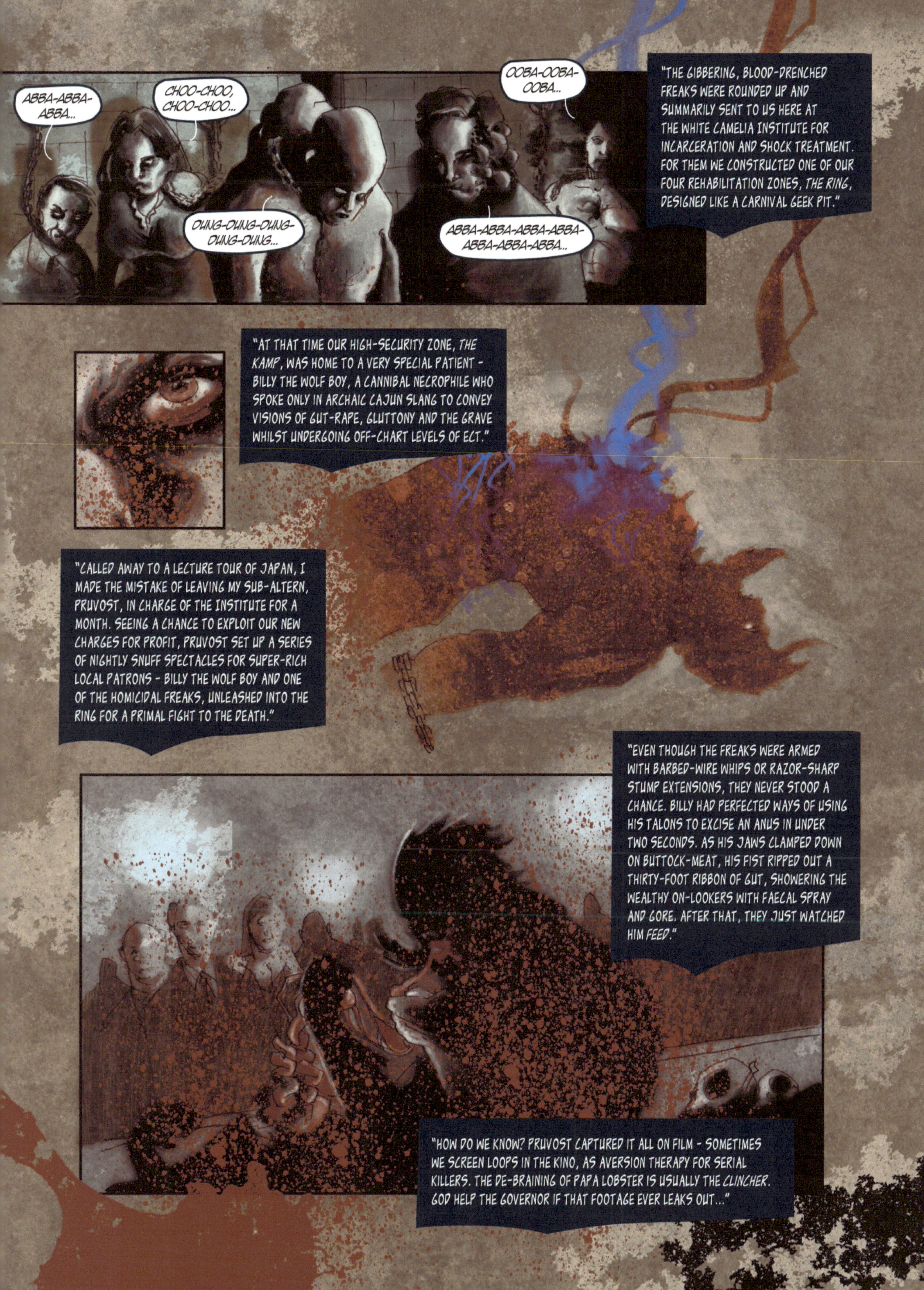

ABBA-ABBA-ABBA...
CHOO-CHOO, CHOO-CHOO...
OOBA-OOBA-OOBA...
DUNG-DUNG-DUNG-DUNG-DUNG...
ABBA-ABBA-ABBA-ABBA-ABBA-ABBA-ABBA...
"THE GIBBERING, BLOOD-DRENCHED FREAKS WERE ROUNDED UP AND SUMMARILY SENT TO US HERE AT THE WHITE CAMELIA INSTITUTE FOR INCARCERATION AND SHOCK TREATMENT. FOR THEM WE CONSTRUCTED ONE OF OUR FOUR REHABILITATION ZONES, THE RING, DESIGNED LIKE A CARNIVAL GEEK PIT."
"AT THAT TIME OUR HIGH-SECURITY ZONE, THE KAMP, WAS HOME TO A VERY SPECIAL PATIENT - BILLY THE WOLF BOY, A CANNIBAL NECROPHILE WHO SPOKE ONLY IN ARCHAIC CAJUN SLANG TO CONVEY VISIONS OF GUT-RAPE, GLUTTONY AND THE GRAVE WHILST UNDERGOING OFF-CHART LEVELS OF ECT."
"CALLED AWAY TO A LECTURE TOUR OF JAPAN, I MADE THE MISTAKE OF LEAVING MY SUB-ALTERN, PRUVOST, IN CHARGE OF THE INSTITUTE FOR A MONTH. SEEING A CHANCE TO EXPLOIT OUR NEW CHARGES FOR PROFIT, PRUVOST SET UP A SERIES OF NIGHTLY SNUFF SPECTACLES FOR SUPER-RICH LOCAL PATRONS - BILLY THE WOLF BOY AND ONE OF THE HOMICIDAL FREAKS, UNLEASHED INTO THE RING FOR A PRIMAL FIGHT TO THE DEATH."
"EVEN THOUGH THE FREAKS WERE ARMED WITH BARBED-WIRE WHIPS OR RAZOR-SHARP STUMP EXTENSIONS, THEY NEVER STOOD A CHANCE. BILLY HAD PERFECTED WAYS OF USING HIS TALONS TO EXCISE AN ANUS IN UNDER TWO SECONDS. AS HIS JAWS CLAMPED DOWN ON BUTTOCK-MEAT, HIS FIST RIPPED OUT A THIRTY-FOOT RIBBON OF GUT, SHOWERING THE WEALTHY ON-LOOKERS WITH FAECAL SPRAY AND GORE. AFTER THAT, THEY JUST WATCHED HIM FEED."
"HOW DO WE KNOW? PRUVOST CAPTURED IT ALL ON FILM - SOMETIMES WE SCREEN LOOPS IN THE KINO, AS AVERSION THERAPY FOR SERIAL KILLERS. THE DE-BRAINING OF PAPA LOBSTER IS USUALLY THE CLINCHER. GOD HELP THE GOVERNOR IF THAT FOOTAGE EVER LEAKS OUT..."

"BILLY'S BLOODLUST WAS IRREVERSIBLE. WHEN THE FREAK MEAT WAS EXHAUSTED, HE TURNED ON PRUVOST. POLICE DISCOVERED HIS MANGLED BODY IMPALED ON THE INSTITUTE'S LIGHTNING-ROD – BUT THEY NEVER FOUND HIS HEAD. AIDED AND ABETTED BY HIS NURSE, CARIL COVEN, BILLY THE WOLF BOY HAD VANISHED INTO THE CHURNING LOUISIANA NIGHT."
IT WAS MY GRANDFATHER, COLONEL ALCIBIADES LE FANU, WHO TRAINED BILLY TO BE THE MAN-SLAYER HE IS.
A NIGGER-EATING ATTACK-DOG OF RELENTLESS RAPACITY AND RAGE.
KINO
RING
AND I WANT HIM BACK.
SET A WOLF TO CATCH A WOLF.... RIGHT, CLETUS?
THE LORD IS MY SHOTGUN, AND I SHALL NOT WANT.
DOLLARS TO DUST, AMEN.

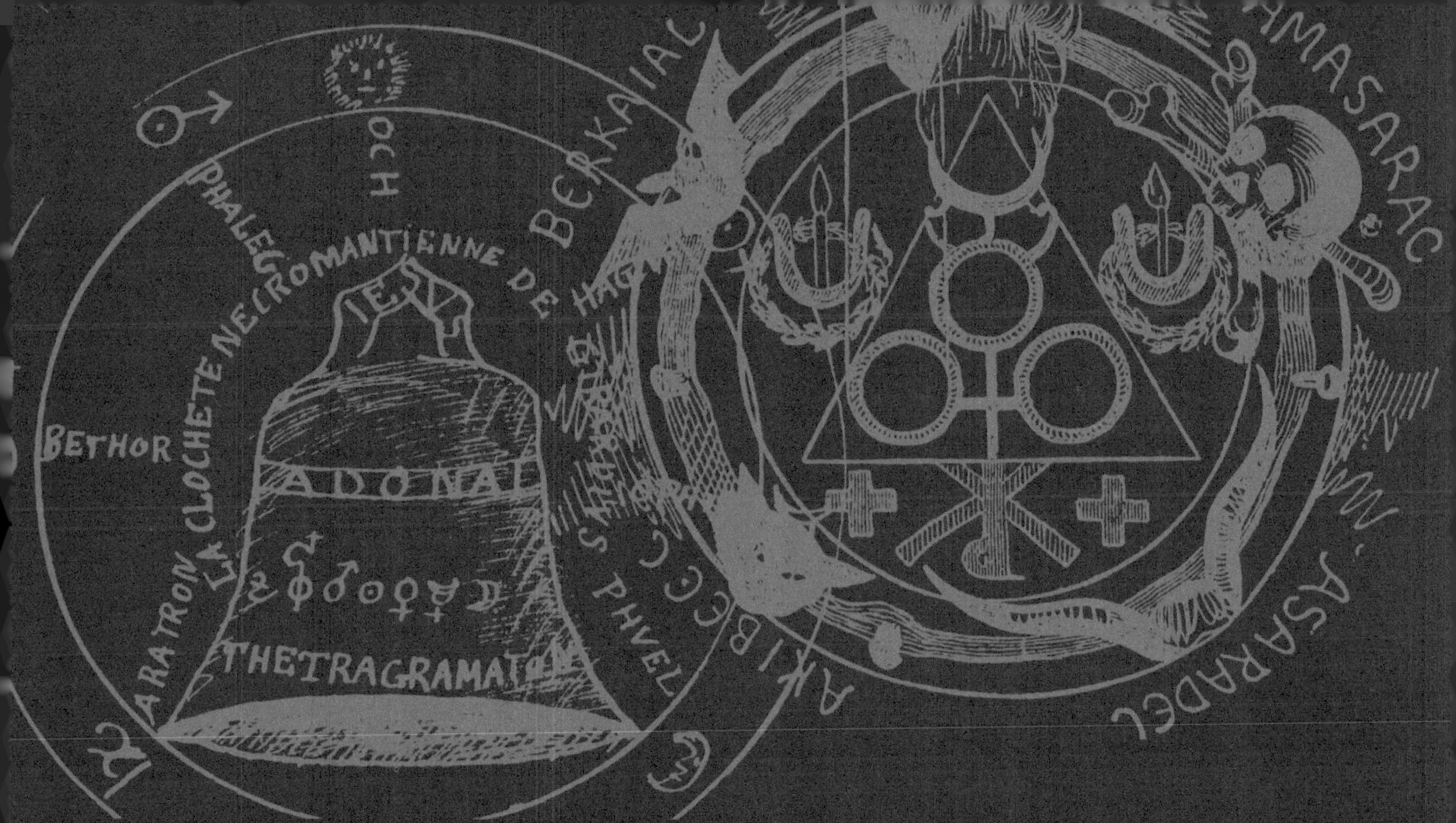

CHAPTER SIX

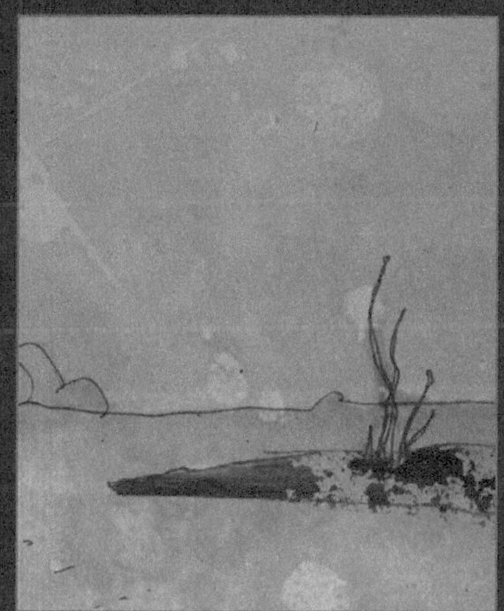

A DEVIL-DOLL SCREAMS IN THE HAUNTED SWAMP

IN THE STORM'S AFTERMATH THE SKY WAS MILK-COLOURED OVER SANDS OF CARCASS TEXTURE, THE SUPPURATING CINNABAR OF A COCKROACH CAUL MANTLED IN LIQUID ICE. BUT IN THE UNRECKONABLE BEYOND THE SUN STILL BOILED WITH INFINITESIMAL VIOLENCE, A SATELLITE RINGED BY VISCID BELTS OF DISSONANCE FROM THE NUCLEUS OF THE RESTLESS BUT IRREFUTABLE UNIVERSE. THE CURVATURE OF SPACE WAS NEGATIVE AND OBLIQUE, PULSARS ETIOLATED TO THE OUTER LIMITS OF TRANSMISSION AFFORDING NO REDRESS. WE HAD LONG SLOUGHED OUR SOULS THE WAY OTHERS JETTISON BAD MEAT.
ON BILLY'S BROW I SAW THE HERETIC CASTE OF THOSE WHO HAVE COMPACTED WITH THE ABYSS. MILLENNIA OF VIOLENCE AND DEPREDATION IN THE EYE CODED SECOND AFTER SECOND. I SAW THAT WAR AND LOVE OF WAR COMPRISED A LITURGY BEYOND ABOLITION IN THE HEARTS OF MEN, THE FIRST STATUTE OF HUMANKIND'S PRIMORDIAL TREATY WITH CHAOS. THOSE WITHOUT ENEMY WARRED AGAINST THEMSELVES, SYNAPSES ERODED BY THE CANCEROUS NOSTALGIAS OF ADDICTION, BONE GRINDING BONE UNTIL THE FINAL DISSOLUTIONS OF THE DITCH. WAR EVEN LIVED IN THE SAP OF ROSES, THE ROSES ON A PAUPER'S GRAVE DESPOILED BY PISSING PANTHERS.
AS DUSK FELL, HIGHWAY AND WILDERNESS INTERLACED LIKE THE SUTURES THROUGH A BARBAROUS CIRCUMCISION AND FROM THE BILIOUS HORIZON TO THE PUCE UNFATHOMABLE VEGETAL REACHES THE SKY DRIPPED DOWN IN ANGUISH. IT WAS MOLTEN CHURCH GLASS SHOT THROUGH WITH A CONFIGURATION OF TOXIC NOVAS, A FISTULAR GLYPTOGRAPH FOR ASSASSINATION. PHANTOMS PASSED. I IMAGINED MY BODY TORN BY AVENGING FANGS, DEVOURED AND REGURGITATED IN A CEASELESS CYCLE AT THE LITHIC TERMINUS OF A GHOST PLANET. MOURNFUL MEMORIES WERE CHASING US DOWN INTO THE UNREPRIEVED CRUX OF A VANISHING-POINT.
THIS WAS BILLY'S SWAMP SHACK, THE OSSUARY WHERE FOR NEARLY A CENTURY HE HAD STRIPPED AND STORED THE DEAD, BURYING MURDER RELICS THE WAY A GUN-BLIND CROW HORDES CHRYSOLITES. IT WAS ANGLED FROM A BAD VOODOO DREAM, AN INVISIBLE AMPUTATION ZONE WHERE ONLY TIMBERWOLVES MIGHT TREAD. THIS WAS OUR ANCESTRAL HOME.
"...LINES WILL APPEAR, THEN NON-SPATIAL GEOMETRIES WILL BE UNDERSTOOD AND PEOPLE WILL LEARN WHAT THE CONFIGURATION OF MIND MEANS AND THEY WILL UNDERSTAND HOW I LOST MY MIND."
DAYS AND NIGHTS PUNCTUATED BY ANTEDILUVIAN SHRIEKS, ZOMBIE SNAKE-CALLS AND THE CHAINSAW CHATTER OF AN AILING DIESEL GENERATOR. IT WAS LONELY WITHOUT YUKI AND CANDICE, BUT SALVATION CAME SOON ENOUGH. A MESSAGE FROM THE AIRWAVES, PRIMING US FOR A DATE WITH PANDEMONIUM.
WE'LL LEAVE YOU WITH A PICTURE OF CANDICE CARRION. IF YOU SEE THIS GIRL, CALL THE FREE NUMBER AT THE BOTTOM OF YOUR SCREEN. THIS WAS PHIL KEEGAN FOR LBC-X, AT THE WHITE CAMELIA INSTITUTE.
LE FANU. WE SHOULD'VE BURNT THAT FUCKING PLACE DOWN WHEN WE LEFT.
IF HE EVER GETS HIS HANDS ON CANDY...
666-666-6666

CLETUS...
WHUT?
YOU EVER FUCKED A PIG?
SAY WHUT?!
C'MON CLETUS... I KNOW YOU WAS DOIN' IT TO OL' MAN WHATELEY'S HEIFER. HOW ABOUT A GOOD OL' SOW, WITH ALL THEM TITTIES?
SHUT THE FUCK UP, LESTER. WE GOT MORE IMPORTANT SHIT TO WORRY ABOUT... LIKE HOW WE'RE GONNA TRAP US A TIMBERWOLF.
SHIT. RECKON WE JUST NEED THE BAIT....
...THEN WE SNARE 'IM, SAME AS WE DONE WITH THAT OL' BUTCHER BOY.
YOU SEE WHAT I SEE?
THAT'S HER, AIN'T IT?
HEADING TO LOUISIANA, MISSY? IT'S YER LUCKY DAY...
...HOP RIGHT IN.
BAYOU LIGHTNING LAND

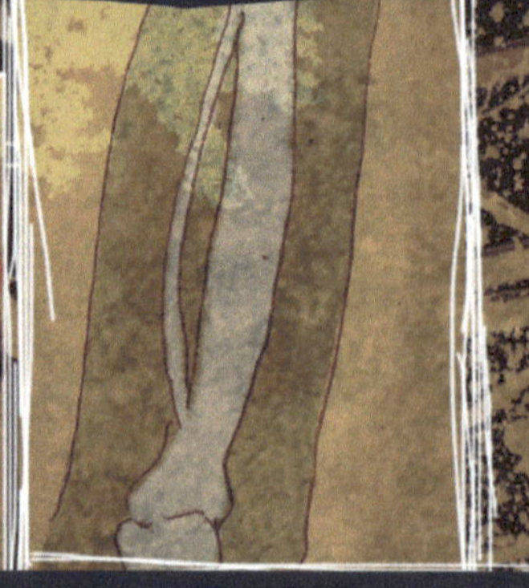

I WAS JUST SEVENTEEN, A TRAINEE PSYCHIATRIC NURSE, WHEN I FIRST CAME TO WORK FOR DOCTOR LE FANU. I ALWAYS REMEMBER HOW HE MOVED AWFUL SLOW, FOR A SKINNY GUY; GUESS YOU COULD PUT THAT DOWN TO MORBID *OBESITY* OF THE *SOUL*. IT WAS LE FANU WHO GAVE BILLY HIS TASTE FOR THE LIGHTNING.

AT THAT TIME I USED TO ASSIST THE DOCTOR ON ALL HIS ELECTRO-SHOCK SESSIONS. FIRST TIME WE DID BILLY, IT WAS A REGULAR DOSE. THE NEXT TIME, LE FANU STARTED CRANKING THE VOLTAGE WAY UP. BUT THE MORE HE HIT HIM, THE MORE BILLY SEEMED TO LIKE IT. HE WAS TALKING AND GROWLING IN SOME KIND OF FRENCH DIALECT, HE HAD A HUGE SMOKING ERECTION, AND THEN HE WENT INTO AN ORGASMIC SEIZURE AND SHOT THE BIGGEST LOAD I EVER SAW. I WAS SO SURPRISED I TRIPPED OVER THE JOLT-CABLES AND FELL RIGHT ON HIM. HIS SEMEN WAS LIKE A SUPER-CONDUCTOR; I SWEAR I COULD SEE THE ARM-BONES DAZZLE NOVA-WHITE THROUGH MY SKIN, I FELT THE CURRENT PUCKER RIGHT UP TO MY SHOULDER, THEN ACROSS MY CHEST AND DOWN INTO MY BELLY AND PELVIC BONES, WHERE IT BUNCHED UP THEN KIND OF EXPLODED ALL TINGLING IN MY INSIDES AND OUT TO MY CUNT-LIPS AND CLIT. THEN I CAME SO HARD THAT THE RED GUSHER STARTED AND BILLY'S EYES FLOWERED UP YELLOW AT THE SCENT OF IT.

GUESS YOU COULD SAY THAT WAS WHEN WE FIRST MADE OUR *CONNECTION*.

NOT LONG AFTER THAT, WE BUSTED OUT OF THE INSTITUTE. NEVER FIGURED WE'D FIND OURSELVES GOING *BACK*.

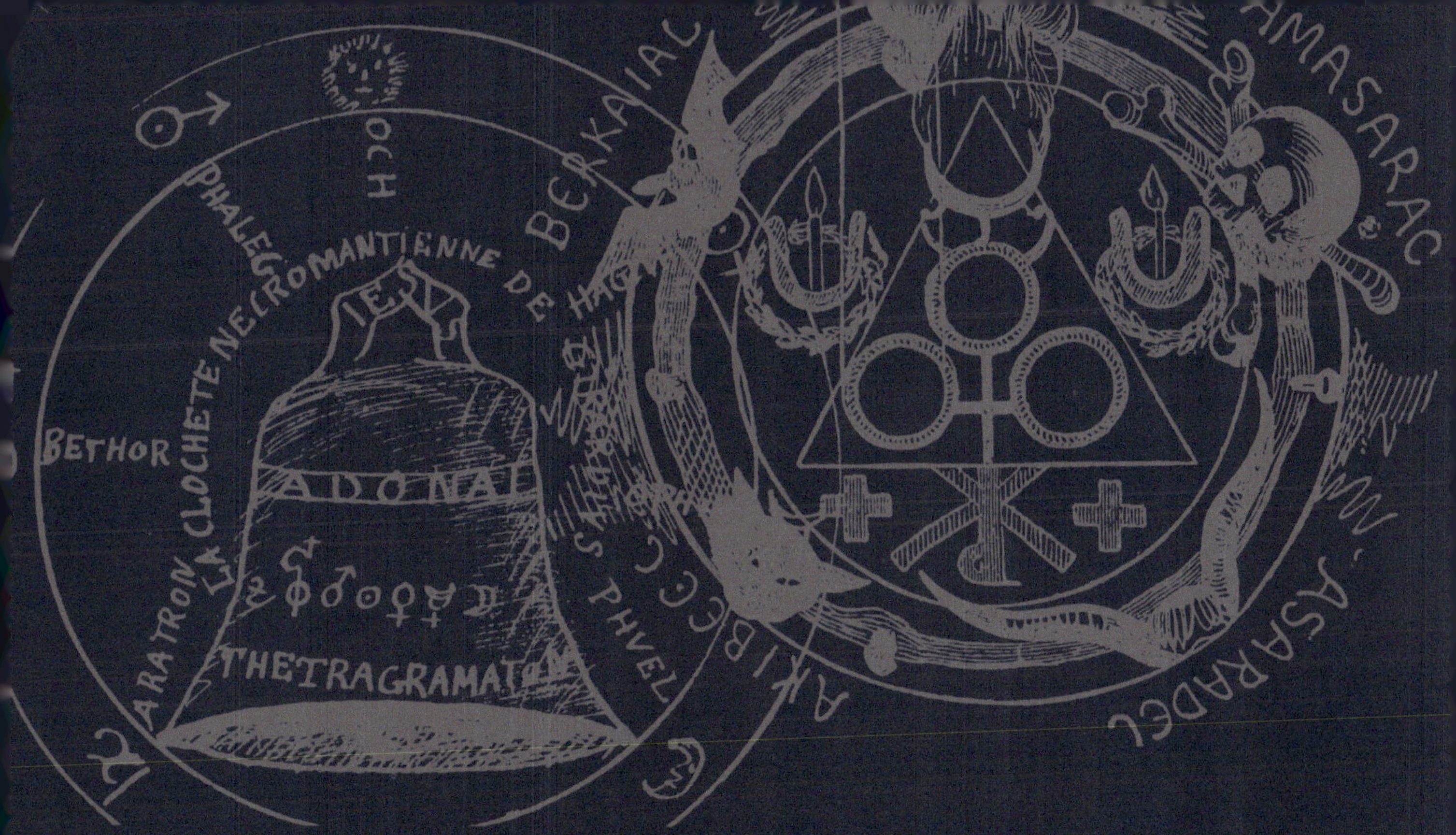

CHAPTER SEVEN

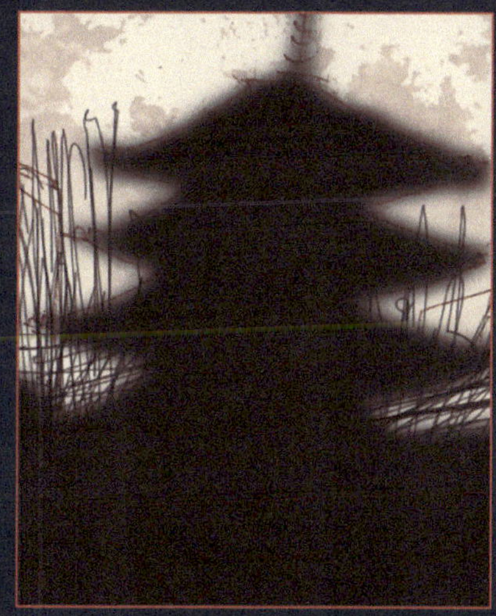

THE RED GIRL FROM THE HOUSE OF DEATH

FOR A WEEK WE DROVE BY NIGHT. PANDORA'S PREDATIONS ON MEN WERE A BIBLICAL ATROCITY. SHE DRANK THEM TO DUST AND LEFT THE HUSKS IN DERELICTION BY THE WAYSIDE.
CAN'T FAULT HER FOR THAT.
HER PURSUIT OF MY AFFECTIONS WAS EQUALLY REMORSELESS.
SEEMS LIKE PANDORA'S SHE-DISCIPLES HAD A COVEN IN EVERY CITY; IN SANTA SANGRE, NEW MEXICO, IT WAS THE SISTERS OF THE PEACOCK PAGODA.
THE PLACE WAS A GLIMMERING PESTHOUSE OF PUTREFIED EYES. THOUSANDS OF THEM, HARVESTED FROM MALE SOCKETS, EMBEDDED IN EVERY FACET OF THE WALLS AND CEILING. CANDLELIGHT LENSED TO INFINITY THROUGH RUPTURED PUPILS AND CRYSTALLIZED RUBY TEARDROPS.
TWO LIBIDINAL TERROR-SLUTS GREETED US IN THE DRIPPING, DELIQUESCENT VESTIBULE.
BELOW, A PENTAGRAM OF TORTURE DUNGEONS WHERE DEATHSHEAD MOTHS LAY EGGS IN THE SKULL-HOLES OF THE SCREAMING BLIND. ABOVE, THE ZODIAC OF GAZES GLISTERS, INFLAMES THE OBSIDIAN ALTAR.
IN THE CHALICE, THE BLOOD AND HOOVES OF THIRTEEN GOATS BORNE BY CRIMSON-COWLED HIEROPHANTS ACROSS A WASTELAND.
QUEEN PANDORA, HOW ABOUT SHOWING ME THE BEDROOM? I NEED TO LIE DOWN, I GOT CRAMPS.
THE THREE MAGIC WORDS.

PANDORA LIKED TO SUCK PUSSY EVEN MORE THAN SHE LIKED TO DRINK BLOOD; AND IF SHE COULD COMBINE THE TWO, SHE WAS HIGH IN REVENANT HEAVEN. I SLIPPED OFF MY PANTIES AND SLOWLY SPREAD MY THIGHS.
THE RED AND THE WHITE, A CONSECRATION TO ETERNITY. YOU GIVE, I TAKE.
SHE SEEMED MESMERIZED; I COULD SEE HER EYES GLAZING OVER, THE DROOL STREAMING FROM HER MOUTH. THERE WERE ANTS IN IT.
I MADE MY MOVE.

NOT SO FAST, LITTLE SUGAR. FIRST YOU MUST SHIT FOR ME; THE DEVIL TAKES HIS DUE. THEN, MY FIST BELONGS INSIDE.

YOU WANT TO FUCK?
I SAID IT BEFORE, I'LL SAY IT AGAIN. AS PANDORA AND HER BITCH-FRIENDS WERE ABOUT TO FIND OUT...

WELL FUCK THIS!!
...THE WAY OF THE SAMURAI IS DEATH.

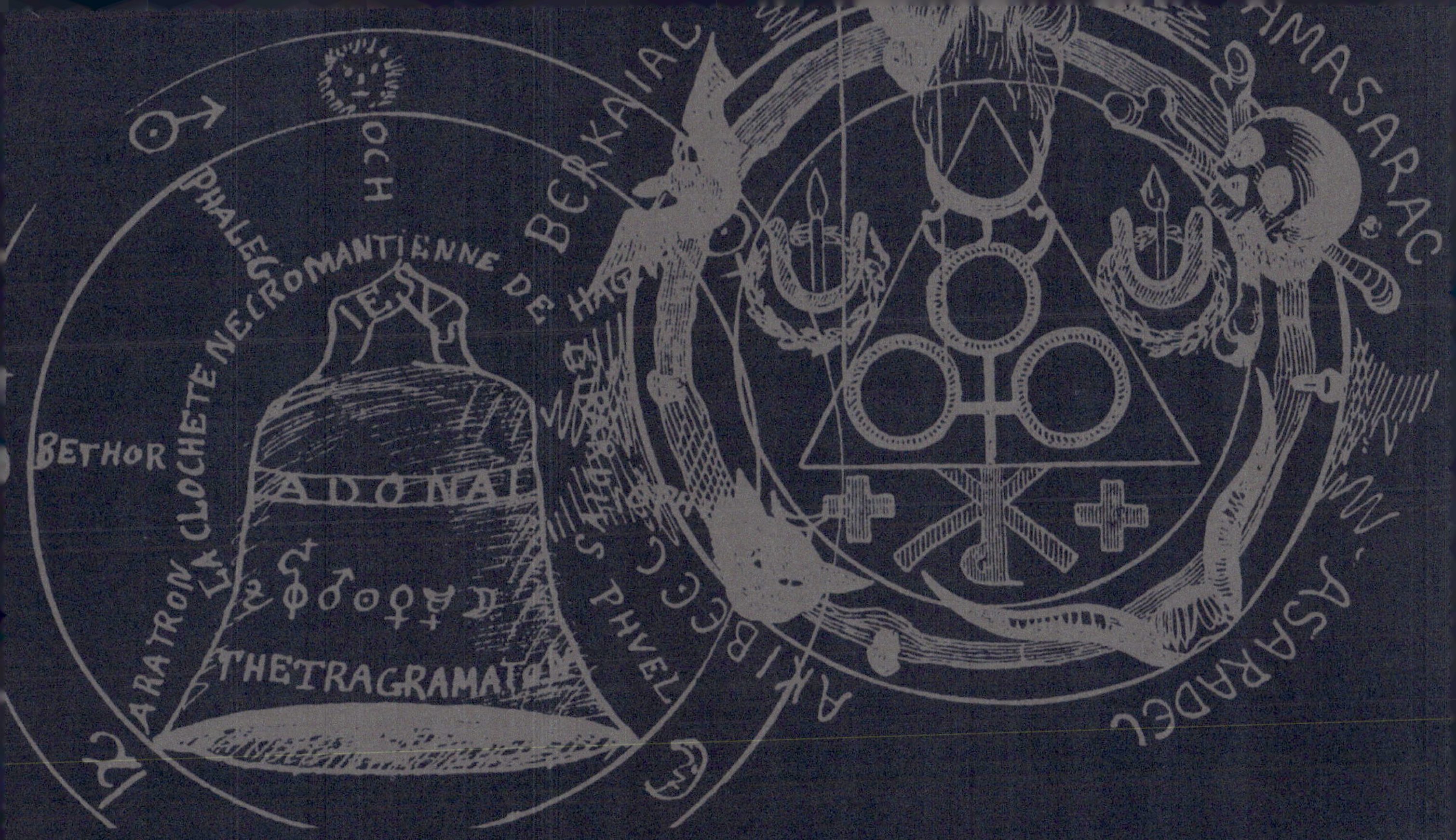

CHAPTER EIGHT

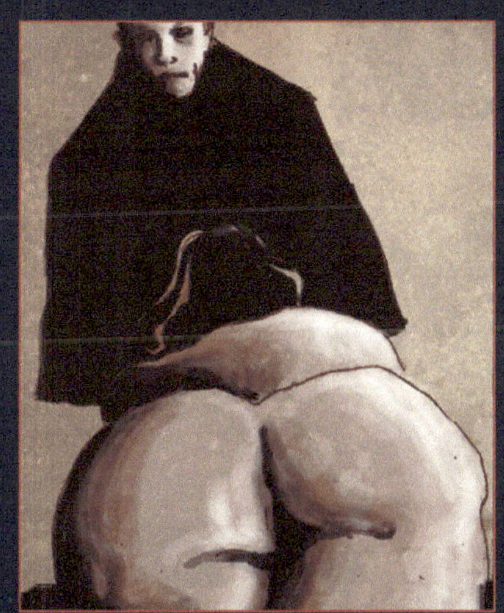

AND THEN THE LIZARD FUCKED THE ROCKING-HORSE

"DEMDYKE WAS ENGLAND'S MOST PROLIFIC SERIAL MURDERER, A SKIPDALE BUTCHER WHO WENT BESERK AFTER A PAKISTANI PROSTITUTE BIT OFF AND SWALLOWED HIS LEFT TESTICLE, CLAIMING IT AS VICTORIOUS REVENGE FOR RADICAL ISLAM AGAINST THE HEATHEN PORK-EATERS. SHE QUICKLY BECAME HIS FIRST VICTIM. DOZENS OF OTHERS FOLLOWED, WHORES WHO HE BRAINED WITH A SLEDGEHAMMER BEFORE DICING THEM AND TURNING THEM INTO LUXURY SAUSAGE - SOME OF WHICH HE IS BELIEVED TO HAVE HAD DELIVERED TO MEMBERS OF THE HOUSES OF PARLIAMENT. THE NEWSPAPERS DUBBED THIS MYSTERIOUS MANIAC 'THE SAUSAGE-MAKER', EVEN SPECULATING THAT HE MIGHT BE THE AVENGING BASTARD SON OF PETER SUTCLIFFE AND A SYPHILITIC STREET-WALKER."

"THEN THE KILLINGS ABRUPTLY STOPPED. IT SEEMS THAT DEMDYKE HAD GONE TO CHICAGO FOR A SLAUGHTERMAN'S CONVENTION AND BECAME ADDICTED TO THE PROSTITUTES FROM THE LOCAL PROJECTS, WHOSE PUNGENT MEAT HE COMBINED WITH CREOLE SPICES TO PRODUCE HIS MOST EXORBITANT SAUSAGES TO DATE. HE WAS FINALLY ARRESTED, DECLARED INSANE, AND SENT TO ME FOR TREATMENT. HE MANAGED TO ESCAPE EN ROUTE, BUT MY BONDSMEN TRACKED HIM DOWN AND RECAPTURED HIM - THOUGH NOT BEFORE HE'D FOUND ONE LAST VICTIM, AN ITINERANT COTTON-PICKER. LACKING HIS USUAL UTENSILS AND INGREDIENTS, THE SAUSAGE-MAKER APPARENTLY IMPROVISED WITH HORRIFIC BRUTALITY, RIPPING OPEN HER BELLY AND DISEMBOWELLING HER WITH HIS BARE HANDS. "

"THEN HE UNRAVELLED HER INTESTINES, TORE OUT A LENGTH THAT WAS FULL OF EXCREMENT, TIED IT OFF AT BOTH ENDS AND TWISTED IT INTO LINKS. HE WAS WEARING THIS ROUND HIS NECK LIKE A TROPHY, UNCOOKED, WHEN WE CAUGHT HIM."

THE INSTITUTE ALMOST LOOKS ALIVE IN THE STORM'S LASCIVIOUS CORUSCATIONS; AND I ALMOST FEEL EXCITED TO BE BACK.

GUESS WE'LL BUST IN THE SAME WAY WE BUSTED OUT - THROUGH THE VAULTS.

A MAZE OF TUNNELS THAT TEEM WITH SQUEALING ALBINO RATS WHOSE EYES HAVE NEVER SUCKED IN STARSHINE, LEADING US TO THE UNDERGROUND EPICENTRE OF THE HOUSE; TWELVE IRON DOORS EMBOSSED WITH MOTHER-OF-PEARL CAMELLIAS, ENCIRCLING A BLACK ALTAR CUT WITH ARCANE PETROGLYPHS AND RANK WITH CURDLED HEART-GORE. THIRTY FEET ABOVE, THE RING.

THE NORTH TUNNEL RISES IN STEADY GRADATIONS, TWISTING BACK ON ITSELF AND SPIRALLING UPWARDS LIKE THE THREAD OF A GRANITE SCREW GAUZED BY CHIROPTERAN SKELETA IN VITREFIED WEBS, ALLUMED BY THE GLOW OF LICHEN THAT CARESSES AND CREEPS. LURING US CLOSER AND CLOSER TO CANDY.

THOSE INSIGNIA... THE TWELVE CARNIVOROUS FLOWERS THAT DREW FIRST BLOOD... STAINS OF AN EVANESCED EVIL FROM A HUNDRED YEARS AGO... A PROTOPLASMIC VESTIGE OF FOETUS-DEVOURING PHANTOMS.

THIS IS THE HOUSE OF BAD SHIT.

WHEN CAN I SEE MY DADDY? YOU PROMISED ME...
NOT LONG NOW, MISSY. WE'RE JUST WAITIN' FER YER FRIENDS TO JOIN THE PARTY.
YOU KEEP A-WRIGGLIN NOW, LITTLE WORM.
I HEAR FOOTSTEPS DOWN BELOW.

WHITE CAMELIA MENTAL INSTITUTE: THE KINO
LADIES AND GENTLEMEN, WE HAVE A NEW GUEST WITH US TODAY - MONSIEUR GUILLAUME GAROU, AKA BRISE-CUL AKA ASS-DESTROYER AKA BILLY THE WOLF BOY AKA BILLY TIMBERWOLF.
WANTED IN THIRTEEN STATES FOR VAGRANCY, GRAVE-ROBBING, CANNIBALISM, MURDER, AND SEVEN HUNDRED COUNTS OF SODOMY WITH A CORPSE.
BUT YOU CAN JUST CALL HIM BILLY.
GLAD TO HAVE YOU BACK, SON. AND DON'T WORRY ABOUT YOUR GIRLFRIEND - WHILE YOU'RE HERE, SHE WON'T BE GOING ANYWHERE. QUELLE JOLIE TITE CATIN...
I AM THE FIRESKIN, AVATAR OF ERZULIE, MOTHER OF MAUSOLEUMS AND THE LEGIONS OF THE LIVING DEAD; MY REAVING SHALL BE RUINOUS AND WITHOUT REPEAL.
I MIGHT EVEN HAVE HER WEAR THE UNIFORM, JUST FOR OLD TIME'S SAKE.
AS FOR YOUR JAPANESE FRIEND, SHE SEEMS TO HAVE GOT LOST IN THE CATACOMBS. MAYBE THE SNOW-RATS GOT HER... OR ELSE THE POX.
NOW THEN - WE'VE GOT A SPECIAL PROGRAM FOR YOU TODAY, DEMDYKE. AND BILLY - I THINK YOU'LL APPRECIATE IT TOO. OTTO MUEHL'S SHIT-BASTARD, FRANJU'S THE BLOOD OF THE BEASTS...
...AND MY FAVOURITE - EDISON'S FUN IN A BUTCHERSHOP.
NURSE HARDY - START THE SHOW.
ENJOY.
BLOOD-BASTARD-BUTCHER, BLOOD-BASTARD-BUTCHER...
I'LL FOOKIN COOK THEE, I WILL.
LE FANU'S THERAPY IS AS GOOD AS IT GETS... WATCHING SEX AND SLAUGHTER REELS WHILE THESE CRAZIES BEAT THEIR MEAT, THEN JACKING UP SOME RAW VOLTS BEFORE FEEDING TIME. SO WHAT'S NOT TO LIKE?
LET THE OLD MAN HAVE HIS FUN FOR A FEW DAYS... BEFORE WE EAT HIS FUCKING HEAD.

BLOOD-BASTARD-BUTCHER! BLOOD-BASTARD-BUTCHER!!

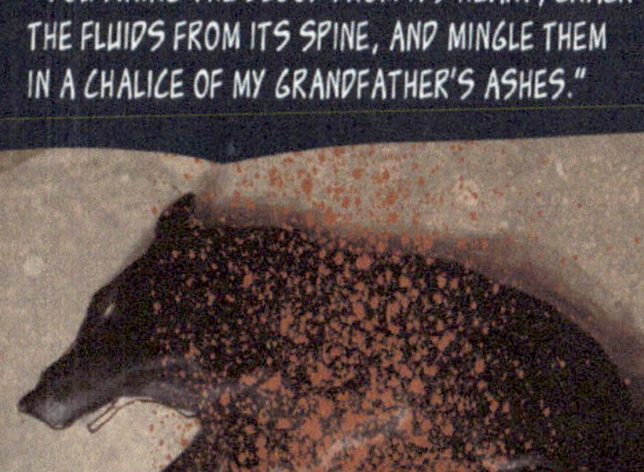

MY MAMA'S DEAD, AND MY DADDY'S CRAZY. THEY'LL NEVER LET HIM OUT OF THIS PLACE NOW... AN INSANE PREACHER, DELIVERING SERMONS TO PSYCHOS IN THE CONVERTED LATRINES OF A LUNATIC ASYLUM. BILLY AND CARIL ARE THE ONLY FAMILY I'VE GOT LEFT NOW.

I BELONG TRULY TO THE TOMBSTONE WRECKAGE, TO THE WAR BETWEEN SHADOW AND SKIN... TO THE MUTANT, MEGA-VOLTAGE TRYST OF THE *TEENAGE TIMBERWOLVES*.

NOTHING LIKE STARTING THE DAY WITH A DOUBLE DECAP.

FIVE DAYS IN THOSE FUCKING SEWERS... SICK TO MY GUTS OF RAT MEAT.
GUESS THAT'S WHY THEY CALL THEM REDNECKS...

SOMETHING I CAN DO FOR YOU, SWEETIE?
HAI.

WHITE CAMELIA MENTAL INSTITUTE: THE RING
THE GOLDEN KNIGHTS ARE RISEN. AND NOW, I CLAIM MY BIRTHRIGHT AS GRANDSON OF OUR FOUNDER, ALCIBIADES LE FANU - MY RIGHTFUL POSITION AS MEGA THERION OF THE KNIGHTS CAMELIA.
AS A MATTER OF FIRST ORDER, ALLOW ME TO READ YOU THE FOLLOWING ENTRY FROM MY GRANDFATHER'S JOURNAL, DATED APRIL 30TH, 1876:
"LAST MIDNIGHT, DURING OUR CUSTOMARY CONVENTION AT THE CIMITIERE LA FITTE, WHERE THE MULATTO WHORES LET US OPEN THEIR VEINS AND SUP IN EXCHANGE FOR YANKEE DOLLARS, WE SUDDENLY HEARD A FRIGHTFUL ERUPTION OF NOISE AND, UPON INVESTIGATION, BEHELD AN APPARITION FROM THE VERY BOWELS OF HELL."

"A LUNATIC BEAST WAS STANDING ASTRIDE THE RIPPED AND MANGLED CORPSE OF A PROSTITUTE, HORROR-HOWLING, SHITTING INTO HER DEAD BELLY AND SHAKING BLOODY BONES IN EITHER FIST, HIS MOUTH A GRIEVOUS SEWER, HIS EYES LIKE PUNCTURES IN A SCROTUM OF BLACK PUS. BY SHEER FORCE OF NUMBERS AND AT PROFUSE GUNPOINT WE MANAGED TO CAPTURE THIS OGRE, AND AS HIS MURDEROUS RAGE SUBSIDED, HE TOLD US HIS NAME WAS BRISE-CUL, ANUS-SPLITTER AND KING OF THE CANNIBAL CRYPT, AND THAT HE WAS ONE HUNDRED AND TWO YEARS OLD."

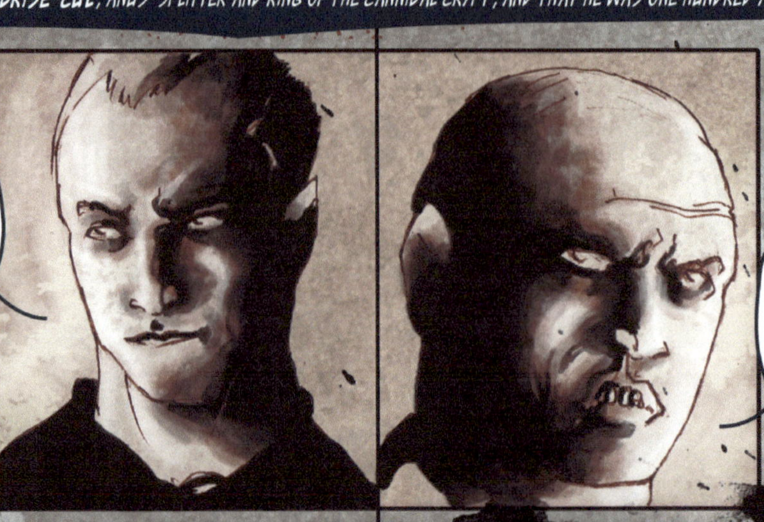

GENTLEMEN: ALLOW ME TO PRESENT THE VERY SAME BRISE-CUL - OTHERWISE KNOWN AS BILLY THE WOLF BOY, THE ONE WHO STACKS MORGUE-MEAT AT THE GATES OF THE INFERNO.
TODAY, FOR YOUR ENTERTAINMENT, BILLY IS PITTED AGAINST AMOS DEMDYKE, MASTER BUTCHER. A FEARSOME SPECIMEN - DESPITE HIS UNFORTUNATE GENITAL MUTILATION...
AYE, WELL, THA KNOWS WHAT THEY SAY, DOCTOR: INT' KINGDOM OF EUNUCHS, THE ONE-BOLLOCK MAN IS KING. I'M THE BASTARD WHO CUT THE CUNT OUT OF SCUNTHORPE, ME.
KILL, CASTRATE, COOK! KILL, CASTRATE, COOK!

"I'LL TAKE YR WHITE NIGGER BREATH AND SMASH IT TO THE BACK WALL OF FUCK," SAYS BILLY TO THE BUTCHER, AND THEN THE BUTCHER'S EYES ROLL BACK LIKE THE SWITCH OF FAECAL PARASITES IN A JUNKYARD AND THE GROUND SHAKES WITH THE CHAMPING OF CHAINS AS IF AN INFERNAL BALLISTIC WAS JUST VOMITED THROUGH A GULLEY AT THE CENTRE OF THE EARTH.
IN THIS SMEARED DETONATION OF SOUND AND VISION, THE BUTCHER'S BLUBBERED FINGERS GROPING INTO BILLY'S LOINS AND TRYING TO RIP HIS COCK-ROOT OUT, SPRAYING SWEAT AND CRUMBS OF DRIED-OUT EXCREMENTS, FRACTURING TEETH IN THE MESH OF MANACLES, APRONS TEARING OPEN SHOWING A HEAVY NIPPLE SCARRED BY CIGARETTE BURNS, BILLY PIVOTING AND POKING HIS FINGER INTO THE BUTCHER'S EAR-DRUM, THE BUTCHER THRESHING, HOODED KNIGHTS OF THE GOLDEN SWASTIKA BAYING FOR DESTRUCTION, BILLY'S TALONS SLASHING TENDER BELLY UNDER RIBCAGE, OPENING FATS FROM NAVEL TO GROIN, FEMORAL ARTERY SPURTING, FIST PLOUGHING INTO GARBLED GASH AND CHOPPING, CUTTING, CARVING SATURATED MEATS AND CAECUM WITH STINK OF CANCERS; SPLIT SPINE VENTING ITS VIRUS CACHE, THE BUTCHER GARGLING BLANKLY INTO PARALYSIS.
COOK THAT.

GIBLETS FOR THE WAR DOGS, SHIT FOR THE SHOVEL. SHOW'S OVER.
NOW WIRE US UP FOR A LAST HIT OF JUICE, BEFORE WE GO.
AND YOU TAKE CARE OF MY DADDY NOW, OK?

A BEAUTIFUL STAR BURNS IN THE PURE WHITE NIGHT, WITH PSYCHO-CATS ON ITS VAPOUR TRAIL. THIS IS THE VELOCITY OF VERMIN IN THE FUR AGE.

...AND RAVAGED INTO RED DUST BY THE CATERWAULING BANSHEES OF THE PRECIPICE...
JUICE? HOW ABOUT SOME OF THE HARD STUFF? SINCE WE GOT OUR STATE LICENSE TO CARRY OUT EXECUTIONS, THINGS'VE HOTTED UP AROUND HERE. WE OPERATE A SCORCHED BONE POLICY FOR IRREMEDIABLE SOCIOPATHS; NO MORE PUSSYFOOTING AROUND WITH ECT, WE GOT US A NEW TOY...
I WONDER IF HIS COCK'S REALLY THAT BIG...
...WE CALL IT THE SKULL-SMOKER.
THINK YOU CAN HANDLE IT?
BRING IT ON.
LET IT FALL IN THE FUNHOUSE SHARDS, LET THE UNIVERSE DROWN IN A HURRICANE OF ELECTRIC BLOOD, LET IT FALL.
TONIGHT, WE SET FIRE TO CIVILIZATION.

WHEN I USED TO WORK HERE, THE RING'S ANTE-CHAMBER WAS A REC ROOM FOR THE CIRCUS FREAKS, SET UP SO LE FANU COULD WATCH BRAIN-DAMAGED DWARFS AND PHOCOMELIANS FUCKING ON CCTV. NOW IT'S RIGGED OUT LIKE SOME *SNUFF-ANNEXE* OF AUSCHWITZ.

A PENAL PROCESSING FACTORY WHERE THE CAMERA'S CONVEX, CONSUMPTIVE EYE IS A HAUNTED HELLSCREEN OF TERMINAL CURSES, A DIORAMA IN WHICH THE DAMNED ARE OBLIVIONIZED IN A FLEETING FLUORESCENCE OF NEURONS.

THIS IS THE POINT OF NO RETURN – THIS IS THE *LIVING END*.

WHEN THEY PUT BILLY IN THAT CHAIR ALL WIRED UP AND WETTED DOWN AND THREW THE SWITCH ON HIM, I WAS SURE HE'D BE RIDING THE LIGHTNING FOR THE LAST TIME, UNEARTHED AND UNEARTHLY, LAUGHING ALL THE WAY TO HELL, AND IT CUT ME DEAD. MY HEART FELT LIKE AN OPEN SORE; I LOOKED OVER AT CARIL. SHE WAS DARK, DARK AS THAT CELL WHERE THEY'D KEPT BILLY, DARK AS A SNUFFED-OUT CANDLE. SHE TREMBLED AS MY DADDY DRONED THE LAST TRANSHUMAN RITES FROM HIS APOCALYPSE OF SPATIAL DEMENTIA.

BILLY ALWAYS SAID THAT THE LIGHTNING WAS ENCODED WITH THE DNA OF DIVINITY ITSELF, AND THAT ONE DAY IT WAS OUR DESTINY TO EMBRACE IT, TO *BECOME* IT WITH BEATITUDE; OUR VERY ANATOMIES *EXCAVATED* BY THE PURGE OF THE *JESUS DEATH FUCK*.

THE JUICE FLAMED ON FULL WITH A HEINOUS RETORT. I SWEAR I COULD SEE BILLY'S ANIMUS MAPPED IN EXTERMINATED EXO-BONE, SEQUESTERED FROM ITS MORTAL HOUSINGS AS IF BY HOLOGRAPHY; AND THEN THE LIGHTS FLEXED OUT INTO NOTHINGNESS AND THEN I SAW NO MORE.

"THESE DISCHARGES, NAUSEA, LASHES. THESE ARE THE THINGS WHERE *FIRE* STARTS. TONGUES AND THEIR FIRE. FIRE WOVEN UP INTO COILED TONGUES IN THE SHIMMERING OF THE EARTH, OPENING UP LIKE A BELLY IN LABOUR, WITH ITS HONEY AND SUGAR BOWELS. ALL THIS SOFT BELLY'S OBSCENE WOUND YAWNS OPEN, BUT THE FIRE GAPES ABOVE IT WITH BURNING, TORTUOUS TONGUES, WITH VENTS AS IF THIRSTING AT THE TIPS..."

"...THIS FIRE ENTWINED LIKE CLOUDS IN LIMPID WATER AND BESIDE IT THE LIGHT DELINEATES A FERRULE AND FILAMENTS. AND THE EARTH HALF-OPEN, EVERYWHERE, REVEALING ARID SECRETS. SECRETS LIKE SURFACES. THE EARTH AND ITS GUTS AND ITS PREHISTORIC SOLITUDE, THE EARTH'S PRIMITIVE FORMATIONS WHERE THE WORLD'S STRATA ARE UNCOVERED IN COAL-BLACK SHADOWS.

"THE EARTH GIVES BIRTH BENEATH THE ICY FIRES. SEE THE FIRE IN *THREE RAYS*, WITH THE CROWNING OF ITS MANE WHERE EYES TEEM. EYES, MILLIONS OF MILLIPEDES OF THEM. THE CONVULSED, INCANDESCENT CENTRE IS LIKE A THUNDERBOLT'S QUARTERED LANCE AT THE FIRMAMENT'S SUMMIT. THE WHITE-HOT CONTRACTING CENTRE. PURE EXPLOSIVENESS IN A CLASH OF POWER. FORCE'S TERRIBLE LANCE WHICH SHATTERS IN TOTALLY BLUE REVERBERATIONS.

"THE *THREE RAYS* FAN OUT, THEIR SPOKES PLUMMET DOWN AND CONVERGE ON THE SAME CENTRE. THIS CENTRE IS A WHITEISH DISH COVERED WITH A SPIRAL OF ECLIPSES.

"THE SHADOWS OF THIS ECLIPSE FORM A BARRIER ON THE ZIG-ZAGS OF THE HEAVENS' TOWERING MASONRY.

"BUT ABOVE THE SKY IS THE *DOUBLE-HORSE*. WHEN CONJURED UP, THE HORSE IS STEEPED IN THE LIGHT OF POWER, ON THE BACKGROUND OF A RAGGED WALL AND CONSTRICTED TO ITS VERY LIGAMENTS. THE LIGAMENT BETWEEN ITS TWIN BREASTS. AND WITHIN IT, THE FIRST OF THESE TWO IS MUCH STRANGER THAN THE OTHER. BRILLIANCE IS CONCENTRATED IN IT, WHILE THE SECOND IS ONLY A HOBBLED SHADOW OF THAT BRILLIANCE.

"LOWER YET THAN THE WALL'S PENUMBRA, THE HORSE'S HEAD AND BREAST FORM A SHADOW AS IF ALL THE WATERS OF THE WORLD RAN UP THE MOUTH OF A WELL WITH THE SPEED OF PROJECTED STARS SLASHED TO THE BONE.

"THE OPEN FAN DOMINATES A PYRAMID OF PEAKS, A VAST HARMONY OF SUMMITS. A HINT OF THE DESERT HANGS OVER THESE SUMMITS AND ABOVE THEM A DISHEVELLED STAR FLOATS, HOVERING, INEXPLICABLY, HORRIBLY. SUSPENDED LIKE THE GOOD IN MAN, OR THE EVIL IN MAN'S RELATIONS TO MAN, OR DEATH IN LIFE, WITH STELLAR ROTATORY FORCE."

EPILOGUE

SHE-WOLF SUPERNOVA

THEY SAY NOT A LOT CAN HAPPEN IN A SINGLE MOMENT...
BUT I'M NOT SO SURE ABOUT THAT.
THE WAY I SEE IT, TIME MAY BE LINEAR, BUT IT MUST ALSO HAVE INFINITE BANDWIDTH. I MEAN, IF YOU ADD TOGETHER ALL THE BILLIONS OF THINGS BEING DONE, SAID, THOUGHT AND DREAMED BY ALL THE BILLIONS OF PEOPLE ON THE PLANET DURING ANY GIVEN MICRO-SECOND...
WELL, YOU GET THE PICTURE.

WHEN THE BUGHOUSE LIGHTS BLEW OUT, LUPINE *NIGHT VISION* WAS THE KEY TO SURVIVAL.

AS I WAS PUTTING PAID TO NURSE KURONEKO HERE, CARIL WAS THROTTLING DOCTOR LE FANU WITH A LOOP OF DEMDYKE THE SAUSAGE-MAKER'S SPILLED-OUT GUTS, WHILE THE GOOD DOCTOR'S GOLDEN HELL-RIDERS STUMBLED AROUND IN THEIR BLACK HOODS, CHOKING ON THE ACRID STENCH OF BRIMSTONE AND BURNT HAIR, AND THE PANICKED SCREAMS OF CAGE-RATTLING INMATES ROSE TO A FRENZIED, CACOPHONOUS CRESCENDO.

SEEMS LIKE BILLY WAS JUST TOO TOUGH TO FRY. HE SOAKED UP WAVE AFTER WAVE OF HIGH-VOLTAGE JUICE, SUCKING IT INTO HIS BALLS BEFORE BLASTING IT BACK IN A HOWLING ORGASMIC SURGE THAT CRACKED LIKE FORKED LIGHTNING, OVERLOADING THE MANSION'S GENERATORS AND PLUNGING ITS SHUTTERED CELLWORKS INTO PRIMEVAL BLACKNESS – BLACKNESS THAT COULD ONLY BE REPRIEVED BY THE INSURGENT FLICKERINGS OF A FIRESTORM. THEN HE BUSTED CLEAN OUT OF THE SMOULDERING EMBRACE OF THE *SIZZLE-SEAT* AND GRABBED HOLD OF CANDICE AS SHE GROPED VAINLY FOR HER DADDY, WHO HAD FALLEN TO HIS KNEES CONVINCED THAT A SOLAR ECLIPSE HAD COME TO PRESAGE THE RITUAL ENUCLEATION OF EVERY HUMAN EYEBALL.

WE LEFT BY THE FRONT DOOR.

BURN, DOGFUCKER, BURN! BURN, DOGFUCKER, BURN!

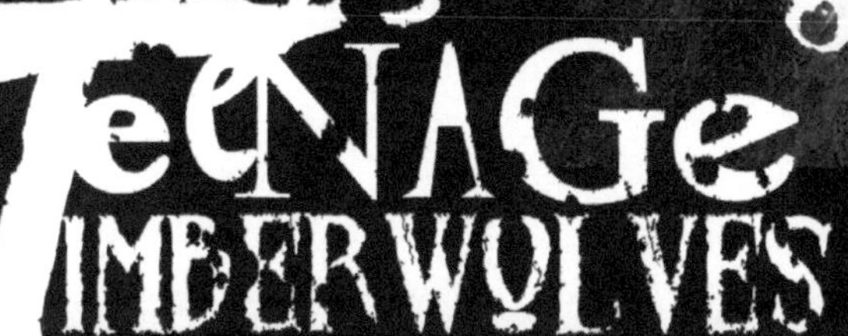

TEENAGE TIMBERWOLVES

BLACK DEAD BONES OF IDIOT BILL

BLOODY BILL WAS A STONE KILLER, A MAN WHO HURLED HIS MOTHER'S MEAT INTO THE CRAB VORTEX AND PLEDGED FEALTY TO THE CREEPING BLIND ONE; HIS MORTAL RELICS ENTOMBED A PINEAL VIRUS TUNED IN TO THE TREADMILLS OF SATAN.
SHOT DEAD BY MILITIAMEN ON OCTOBER 26, 1864, BLOODY BILL WAS DRAGGED THROUGH THE STREETS AND BURIED IN AN UNMARKED GRAVE IN PIONEER CEMETERY, RICHMOND. FROM THIS DITCH I BORE HIS PESTILENTIAL BONES TO MONUMENT.
IMAGINE A COVEN OF CANNIBAL GASH CASTING GRISTLE SEWER-DEEP IN DEMENTIA, FED ON THE DARK ROASTED CARCASS CRAWLING WITH CORNEAL PARASITES, PROCLAIMING DEVOTION TO DEATH AND KILL AND ALL KIN THEREOF.
IMAGINE THE ONES WHO BOIL BLOOD THAT IT MUST BEND AND ABIDE BY THEIR SIGHTLESS RETRIBUTIONS.
THESE ARE THE IDIOT BRIDES OF AZATHOTH.

VIRGIN BLOOD SACRIFICE, ORGIASTIC SEX MAGICK AND INVOCATIONS TO AZATHOTH RESTORED LIFE AND FLESH TO BLOODY BILL'S HEAD, WHICH BECAME THE AVATAR OF THE SCOURGE. LAPAGE AND HIS SHE-DEVILS WOULD ENTER INTO VOODOO TRANCES AND RECEIVE PSYCHIC MESSAGES FROM THIS RESURRECTORY SUMMATION.

SHADOWS OF SODOMY, MISCEGENY AND BESTIALITY IN GUTTERVILLE: SUDDEN SNAP OF THEIR CRUSH WITH A SHARK AT TREES: THE MARSH STRAYED SO FAR FROM MYSTERY: LEAVES ARE SOFTLY MOVING: THEY BARK AT SPIDERS INTELLIGENT EYES: THEY SCUTTLE UP TREES TO LONG LEGS AND WHISPER SUSPENDED BETWEEN NOTHING TO BARK AT CROWS THAT ESCAPE THEM: PERCHES WITH TIRED INCH RETURN TO EAT ALL DAY: ON THE SHORE THEY BARK AT THE ROCKS ON THE WINGS: THEY BARK AT TOP OF MASTS APPEARING AT THE NAVIGATION LIGHTS: SOUND OF THE WAVES BARK AT THE MUFFLED INVISIBLE SHIPS: THE BLACK BACK WHILE THE FISH THAT SHOWS: THEY BARK AT THE HUNGRY ABYSS AND THEY BARK AND SINK INTO THE ABYSS SWIMMING: THEN THEY START TO RUN THEM: AFTER THE MAN WHO ENSLAVES RUNNING AGAIN THROUGH THE COUNTRY ON BLEEDING PAWS TO THE ROCKS: GRASS AND STENCH OVER PITS, PATHS, FIERY ROCKS: YOU WOULD BE RABID AND SEARCH AND THINK THEY WERE A VAST POND OF THIRST: THEY QUENCH THEIR RAGING PROLONGED HOWLS TERRIFYING TRAVELLERS NATURES: THE WAND SHOULD BEWARE: THOSE MYSTERIES WILL THROW FREQUENTERS OF CEMETERIES INTO THEMSELVES UPON HIM, RING WITH THEIR BLOOD TEARING AND DEVOURING DRIPPING JAWS: OTHER SAVAGE THEY HAVE STRONG TEETH CREATURES: WILL NOT DARE THE BLOODY FLESH, BUT APPROACH AND SHARE IT WILL FLEE FROM SIGHT: SEVERAL HOURS THEY DO TREMBLING: AFTER SIEGES, ALMOST DEAD WITH RUNNING HERE AND EXHAUSTION FROM THERE, THEIR TONGUES MOUTHS ATTACK LOLLING FROM THEIR ONE ANOTHER WITHOUT ADO AND TEAR EACH KNOWING INTO A THOUSAND SPEEDS: THE PIECES DO NOT ACT WITH GLASSY CRUELTY.

SO DID BLOODY BILL DICTATE THE SEVEN SONGS OF AZATHOTH IN THE CRYPT OF THE SCOURGE OF THE BURNING SKULL-VIRGINS; AND AFTER TWENTY-THREE DAYS AND NIGHTS OF THE WHITE DARKNESS, LEONARD LAPAGE AWOKE WITH MASSACRE IN MIND.

AND SO THE DAY OF RECKONING CAME. THE SCOURGE RODE INTO THE TOWN OF GUTTERVILLE, LOUISIANA AND RAZED IT TO THE GROUND AND BUTCHERED EVERY MAN, WOMAN, CHILD AND BEAST THEREIN, UNTIL NOTHING TWITCHED SAVE SCORPIONS UNDER BOOT-HEELS AND THE SUN WEPT TEARS OF MOLTEN MISERY ACCORDED BY THE ULULATIONS OF BILL.
I SAW HORSES AND RIDERS GYRATE IN A WHIRLWIND OF PULVERISED TRIPES AS BLOOD LAPPED AT THE WALLS OF SANITY; BY MY OWN HANDS SOME FIFTY LAY TORN APART AND I DELIVERED THEIR KIDNEYS TO LAPAGE STRUNG TOGETHER IN VISCID RED SWASTIKAS, SOFT AND SECRET PASS-KEYS TO THE SEVEN GATES OF HELL.
BABY GUTS ON FIRE... THEY KEEP CALLING ME...
A GREAT CANNIBAL FEAST RAGED FOR DAYS AND NIGHTS, LEAVING ONLY BONES BEHIND; GUTTERVILLE WAS ERASED FROM HISTORY;
LAPAGE DISCHARGED ME OF MY DEBT; I WAS FREE TO PURSUE THE BLOOD-FREEZING SWERVES OF THE MOON.
PER ARDUA, AD FOSSAM! KILL KILL KILL!!

DANIELE SERRA IS AN ITALIAN ILLUSTRATOR AND COMIC BOOK ARTIST. HIS MAIN INFLUENCES AND INSPIRATIONS ARRIVE FROM WEIRD AND HORROR FICTION WRITTEN BY H. P. LOVECRAFT AND WILLIAM H. HODGSON, RIDLEY SCOTT MOVIES, JAPANESE HORROR FILMS AND CLIVE BARKER'S WORKS.

HIS LOVE FOR HORROR CULTURE STARTED BEFORE HIS PAINTING CAREER, MAKING HIM QUICKLY DEVELOP HIS SIGNATURE STYLE: HIGH CONTRAST PAINTINGS WITH BRIGHT, AS WELL AS STRONG DARK COLORS, CURVED STROKES AND SHADOWS, AND A PARTICULAR ATTENTION TO HIS CHARACTER'S GAZE AND EXPRESSION.

AS A COMIC BOOK ARTIST DANIELE WORKED FOR IMAGE COMICS [FADE TO BLACK, WRITTEN BY JEFF MARIOTTE], BOOM! STUDIOS, [CLIVE BARKER'S HELLRAISER: BESTIARY], TITAN COMICS [DARKSOULS], IDW PUBLISHING [THE CROW: MEMENTO MORI, WRITTEN BY MICOL BELTRAMINI], SERAPHIM INC. [CLIVE BARKER'S HELLRAISER ANTHOLOGY VOLUMES 1 AND 2, BOTH COVERS AND INTERIOR ART].

IN 2014 DANIELE WORKED WITH WORLDWIDE BESTSELLING AUTHOR JOE R. LANSDALE, ON THE GRAPHIC NOVEL "I TELL YOU IT'S LOVE" FOR SHORT, SCARY TALES PUBLICATIONS. DANIELE'S ILLUSTRATIONS HAVE BEEN INCLUDED IN BOOKS BY STEPHEN KING AND RAMSEY CAMPBELL AND HE PROVIDED THE ART FOR GRAPHIC NOVELS WORKING WITH AUTHORS LIKE CLIVE BARKER, MARCELLO FOIS AND OTHERS.

IN 2018 DANIELE WORKS ON "TOMMYKNOCKERS" BY STEPHEN KING [PS PUBLISHING], PROVIDING THE ART FOR ALL THE THREE WRAPAROUND COVERS, THE INTERIOR ILLUSTRATIONS AND THE BOXSET.

DANIELE'S WORKS INCLUDE OVER 250 BOOK COVERS FOR PUBLISHERS FROM ALL AROUND THE WORLD, MOST NOTABLY: "THE BIG BLOW" BY JOE R. LANSDALE, "VOICES FROM THE BORDERLAND" BY WILLIAM HOPE HODGSON, "HELLRAISER: THE TOLL" BY ALAN MILLER, "DEEP LIKE THE RIVER" BY TIM WAGGONER AND "FRANKENSTEIN IN LONDON" BY BRIAN STABLEFORD AS WELL AS ARTWORKS FOR VARIOUS MUSIC RELEASES, LIKE: "IX" BY SHINING, "MADMAN — SZPITAL BOX" BY :WUMPSCUT: AND "LAURESTINE" BY SO HIDEOUS, AND ALSO THE COVER OF THE LIMITED DELUXE EDITION OF THE "NIGHTBREED: THE CABAL CUT" BLU-RAY.

DANIELE'S ILLUSTRATIONS HAVE BEEN USED AS THE SET DRESSING OF THE FILM ADAPTATION OF STEPHEN KING'S "CELL" DIRECTED BY TOD WILLIAMS AND STARRING JOHN CUSACK AND SAMUEL L. JACKSON.

JAMES HAVOC WAS A WRITER OF EXPERIMENTAL HORROR FICTION. HIS COLLECTIONS "SATANSKIN" AND "WHITE SKULL" ARE CURRENTLY AVAILABLE THROUGH INCUNABULA.